Bloo
Out and Other
Strange Tales

Blood Will Out and Other Strange Tales

David Rudd

First published by Shakspeare Editorial, November 2024

ISBNs   pbk 978-1-7384422-2-5
         ebk 978-1-7384422-3-2

Illustrations by Duncan Rudd

Design and typesetting www.ShakspeareEditorial.org

To Sheena, Duncan & Sophie

To their partners, Vanessa & Phil

And to our grand-teens, Erin & Felix

Contents

Acknowledgements

My gratitude goes to the following magazines for publishing earlier versions of these works. To *Scribble* for "Vampire in Whitby" and "Falling Fast"; to *Tigershark* for "A Hint of Complicity"; to *Bewildering Stories* for "Loco Pete's Leap" and "Lithe Spirit"; to *The Horror Zine* for "Girl in Room 39"; to *Corner Bar Magazine* for "Strait is the Gate"; to *The Blotter* for "On the Threshold" and "Fear of Flying Freehold"; to *Literally Stories* for "The Fall and Rise of Albert Palmerson"; to *Shorts Magazine* for "The Night Mare"; to *Dissections* for "The Gibbet Tree"; to *Every Day Fiction* for "Rest in Peace"; to *East of the Web* for "RIP"; to *Café Lit* for "The Tale Spinner"; and to *Aphelion* for "Blood will Out" and "Ghost Writer". They are all small magazines deserving public support.

Also deserving mention are Matthew G. Rees (for his much missed e-zine *Horla*, which published several of the above stories early on) and Daniel Bazinga (of *Argosy*, who initially requested more of Jack's adventures in "Blood Will Out").

Finally, thanks to Alison Shakspeare, for making this collection a reality; and to my son, Duncan, for the visual magic he's worked into this book.

Blood Will Out

I

It had been a hectic day for Jack, careering from one side of London to the other, delivering messages, collecting and depositing packages, visiting embassies and clubs. Not that Jack was ever invited into any of these swanky places. He rarely progressed beyond their vestibules (as he'd learnt to call them). In fact, he was more commonly shown the tradesman's entrance.

Now, back at his lodgings, Jack and his fellow errand boys were enjoying a juicy stew provided by Mrs Jade, their landlady. They were comparing notes on the day. As she brought in a plate of bread and butter and a pot of steaming tea, there was a knock at the front door. She went to answer it, returning with a cream-coloured envelope bearing a wax seal, which she ceremoniously handed to Jack.

He was dumbfounded. It was the sort of thing he delivered to others! The cursive script, spelling out his name and address, was rich with loops and flourishes. Everyone round the table looked impressed.

With his own attempt at a flourish, Jack licked clean his knife and, as he had seen others do, slit open the envelope. Inside was a letter on embossed paper from a firm of solicitors called Tumbler and Cumbersome. Jack read it aloud – the only way he knew how. The letter requested the presence of Mr John Arthur Carmel – the others cooed – at the firm's offices in Monument Street. Jack was expected to attend on the morrow at noon, "concerning a matter that should be to his advantage." They cooed louder.

"Very mysterious," said Bob, Jack's roommate. "Come into some dough, 'as we?" The others hooted while Bob started poking Jack.

❦❀❦

Jack reported to the solicitor's offices in plenty of time. He had delivered the morning's messages with more than usual alacrity, thereby managing to extend his half-hour lunch break. Breathless, he sat in the firm's anteroom until invited into Mr Cumbersome's chambers. For Jack, this was progress indeed: moving beyond the vestibule into the inner sanctum.

The plush carpet slowed his progress, but it did give him time to take in the opulence of his surroundings: the book-lined walls, the silk drapes and glass cabinets; and, right in the centre, the biggest desk Jack had ever seen, behind which sat one of the smallest men Jack had ever encountered.

As Jack let the atmosphere soak in, Mr Cumbersome reached across the desk to shake Jack's hand. Jack had to stretch considerably. The secretary, who had shown Jack into the room, returned to his own, much smaller desk just inside the door.

"Well, Mr John Arthur Carmel," began Mr Cumbersome, steepling his hands in front of his chest, "I presume you are wondering what this is all about." Jack nodded vigorously. "Perhaps if I start with your full name."

"You just did, Mr Cumbersome," said Jack.

"Ah, well. In point of fact, no," responded Mr Cumbersome, confirming Jack's view of how he'd always imagined lawyers speaking. "In truth, it's John Arthur Carmello, isn't it?"

"How d'you know that sir?" Jack was impressed.

"Your grandfather decided to change the family name when he fled from his home country, Italy, in the 1860s, didn't he?"

Jack had heard this story before but never been too sure of its accuracy, although he knew he was of Italian stock: his complexion and slight build gave him away.

"Let me cut to the chase, my lad," said Cumbersome, sounding quite avuncular. "You, apparently, are one of the last surviving descendants of an Italian aristocrat, Count Enrico Giuliani. You are not a legitimate descendant but, as the Italians express it, a *bastardo*. That is, you – or rather your father – was born, as they say, the wrong side of the blanket."

"My late father," added Jack. "He died a while back."

Mr Cumbersome nodded sympathetically, indicating that he was aware of this. What the solicitor was saying certainly chimed with tales Jack had heard from his grandparents. However, the more Mr Cumbersome talked, the more outlandish the story became. It sounded like something from one of Jack's penny dreadfuls.

Over the last few generations, Mr Cumbersome explained, the Giuliani family had suffered a number of tragic losses, "reputedly associated with the family curse". Despite uttering this final word with some disdain, he continued using it, as though it were an acceptable legal term.

Apparently, a great aunt had recently died. But Alfonso, who was due to inherit (he would be the next count when he came of age), had disappeared, which is how Jack came to be involved. For, amongst the great aunt's papers, it mentioned the "Carmello connection". Jack, explained Mr Cumbersome, could be a benefactor of the estate.

The aunt was to be entombed at the Giuliani mausoleum, located on a hillside outside Verona, in ten days' time, when there would also be a formal reading of the will. Mr Cumbersome, whose practice had, for a long time, represented the Italian family's English interests, suggested that he accompany Jack across the continent in order to attend the proceedings.

Jack was dumbstruck, but managed a nod of agreement. Given such news, many people would not have returned to work. Jack, however, went back to delivering packages. The work made him feel secure as his mind struggled to come to terms with this potential change to his circumstances. "Count Jack Carmel," or even "Count Jack Carmello". He liked the sound of that!

❆

While Jack worked his week's notice, Mr Cumbersome made the necessary arrangements: obtaining a passport and visa for Jack, booking their passage on the Dover train, the ferry across to Calais and, finally, the Continental express to Verona Porto Nuova.

On the journey, Jack gradually adjusted to this new way of life: remembering to hand his bags to porters rather than carrying them himself, remembering not to stand aside for others and, especially, remembering not to bow and scrape to those he had always considered his betters. Mr Cumbersome was a great help in building Jack's confidence, especially when it came to dining. He introduced Jack to the various bits of cutlery and glassware that crowded a dinner table, explaining how each was deployed. He also showed Jack how food was conveyed to the mouth, chewed, then swallowed.

By the time the Italian border was reached, Jack was feeling reasonably self-assured. And, when the two of them eventually arrived at the Stazione di Verona hotel, Jack thought himself quite the gentleman. He even enjoyed being fitted for a suit specially tailored for him. His measurements had been taken in London and conveyed to a local outfitter, who came to the hotel to oversee the fitting.

But all Mr Cumbersome's careful preparations were upset just before the two of them were due to board a horse-drawn carriage for the Giuliani mausoleum. A much larger man with a pencil-line moustache approached Mr Cumbersome. Jack, assuming it was a local, was surprised to hear a deep English voice declare: "I'll take over now, Cumbersome."

Jack looked to his solicitor, expecting him to protest but, after a few seconds, his face settled into a smile. "Of course," he acceded. Turning to Jack, he introduced the new figure: "I don't believe you've met my partner, Mr Tumbler."

"Senior partner," muttered the latter, loosening his grip on Mr Cumbersome's arm and offering his hand to Jack.

"Mr Tumbler didn't expect to be needed in Verona for this event," added Mr Cumbersome, "but then something came up and, well … the Giulianis are his clients really, so I'll leave you in his, ah, capable hands."

They were certainly very large hands. Jack had watched with concern as his small fingers disappeared into Tumbler's capacious fist.

The next thing Jack was aware of was Mr Cumbersome's receding figure as their carriage picked up pace, moving through Verona's streets.

Not another word was spoken. The carriage was too noisy to conduct any meaningful conversation, but Jack had expected a few pleasantries at least. Mr Cumbersome had drilled him in such small talk, and Jack was keen to exercise his new accomplishment. Mr Tumbler's taciturn form, however, deterred interaction of any sort. He filled the seat opposite Jack. The longer Jack sat there, the more he felt like a mere errand boy again, all Mr Cumbersome's careful preparations undone.

Jack contented himself by attending to the landscape, watching the carriage slowly climb out of Verona up into the scented air and surrounding hills. Now and again, Jack thought he could hear another carriage behind them, but decided it must be their own vehicle echoing through the hills. Had he been with

Mr Cumbersome, he would have sought clarification. Not from this man, though, whose eyes were closed, his posture stiff.

Eventually they reached a clearing where the carriage came to a halt amongst other vehicles, their drivers gathered under a tree. They had arrived at the mausoleum, an imposing, once-white structure that stood majestically on a rocky outcrop. A few other, smartly dressed figures were just emerging from the impressive wooden doors, amongst whom Jack spotted a priest in vestments.

"Good," pronounced Mr Tumbler, speaking for almost the first time. "The service has finished. Just the will, then."

They went inside where, under the guidance of an official, a number of people were arranging themselves around a trestle table that had just been erected in the main chamber. Jack had not been introduced to anyone and was unsure what was going on, as the entire proceedings were conducted in Italian. However, as Mr Tumbler was looking after Jack's interests, he didn't really mind. He took a seat alongside the lawyer and studied the disparate group that had come together in these bizarre surroundings.

It was an intimidating space, with the various nooks and crannies causing the candles to cast elaborate, eerie shadows, as though the whole interior was pulsing with incipient life. There were urns, coffins, caskets and funeral plaques everywhere, with two, more elaborate recesses – separate chambers – leading off the main vaulted space. No doubt, thought Jack, these were where the more illustrious family members were housed.

The omnipresence of death made Jack shudder. It was not a place he'd like to be left alone in. But worse than the monuments themselves was a frieze that ran along one of the outer walls, from floor to Jack's eye level, about five feet high. The carvings depicted images of hell: warnings of the torments that would be inflicted on the unprepared. It was obviously a message to the living rather than to those housed within, for whom it was too late.

Jack was fascinated by the grimacing faces with their vacant eye sockets, toothy grins and snakelike hair. One carving, of a man with a malevolent sneer, especially drew Jack's eye. Despite the absence of eyeballs, the figure seemed to be returning Jack's stare. Like portals opening onto an endless nothingness, the sightless sockets seemed to draw Jack in.

He had little awareness of how long he sat there, watching papers being shuffled, listening to the incomprehensible voices echoing round the vault. But suddenly, the reading seemed to be over, and people were coming up to him, shaking him by the hand and saying a few words before filing out.

Jack found himself alone in the vault with Mr Tumbler, while a few functionaries collapsed the table and removed chairs and candles. Mr Tumbler was gathering his papers, taciturn as ever. Jack presumed that he would be informed of the outcome shortly. In the meantime, he took a closer look at the interior, keen to show an interest, even if he was only a *bastardo*.

As Jack approached the casket of the most recent addition, reputedly his great aunt, he suddenly found himself plunged into darkness. Someone had closed the entrance doors. Jack called out to Mr Tumbler, but he too seemed to have disappeared. Only one candle remained, wanly flickering. Jack started to panic. Where had the doorway gone?

Sweat began to trickle down his back as a nightmare from his boyhood surfaced; something he hadn't thought about in years. In this dream, a spectral hand would systematically extinguish the lights of the family home, until Jack found himself stumbling around in the dark, calling for his parents. Then, just as he thought he was going to suffocate, his mother's voice would finally find his ear. "It's alright, Jack," she would say, and he would wake to find her bending over him, stroking his face.

Smoothing down his hair, Jack realised he was trying to recreate her comforting touch. He made his way across to the lone, flickering candle and removed it from its sconce, careful not to disturb the wan flame. Stumbling round the chamber, he tried to locate the doorway.

Being left in this space, alone, was terrifying enough, but then, more chillingly, he realised he was far from alone. Albeit in differing stages of decomposition, many others were present, including his recently departed great aunt. Moreover, because he shared their blood, he also realised that, in some strange way, this might be where he belonged.

With mounting panic, Jack clawed his way along the wall until he encountered the stone frieze, which, as he remembered, ran along the outer wall. In one direction, he knew it had to lead to the door. He moved his hand over the immobile figures as he stumbled along, hoping to discover the entranceway. These carved beings had been hideous enough to gaze upon, but their touch, rough beneath his hand, was worse. They felt more substantial and real.

Jack's probing hand involuntarily withdrew as he realised he'd encountered the man with the sneer. His fingers had been tracing the wormlike lips, curling back from the granular teeth that encircled the mouth cavity before he comprehended who it was. Tentatively, he reached out again, thinking he'd moved beyond this figure. But somehow it still lay beneath his hands: the slightly upturned nose leading into those hungry eye sockets, which seemed to swallow Jack's probing fingers. They felt bottomless. He hastily withdrew his hand, for his touch seemed to have aroused the figure. Unlike the rest of the frieze, it now felt warm, as though it had come alive within the stonework. Jack envisaged this granular figure as having once been human and, somehow, had become trapped within the frieze.

At this disturbing thought, Jack tried to push himself away from the ravening frieze, but his left hand was suddenly arrested, stone fingers clamping his wrist. He was momentarily petrified as he imagined himself experiencing the very fate he'd just been picturing. But, as he then realised, rather than trying to drag him into the stone, this figure seemed to be using Jack's arm for leverage, as though seeking to work itself free of the stone. Jack felt the creature's thumb over his pulse, envious, perhaps, of his animated condition.

Several things then happened simultaneously. Jack moved the candlestick so that he could view his manacled wrist more clearly. As he did so, hot wax guttered onto it. The pain nearly made him drop the candle but, somehow, he managed to sustain the quivering flame. But, as he could now more clearly see, it was not just hot wax that pained him. Blood was oozing from his wrist, albeit staunched by the hand that clamped him, providing an effective tourniquet.

Jack initially thought he might have inflicted this wound on himself, gashing his wrist when he'd jerked his hand away from the wax. But he then realised he'd been bitten! And with that recognition came a fear of vampirism. At the time, Dracula was all the rage in London, and Jack and Bob often pretended to be members of the undead, standing in front of the mirror comparing canines.

However, though Jack now braced himself for some real bloodletting, nothing else happened. The hand released his wrist and, in that instant, the figure appeared to slump back into the frieze.

With a gust of wind, the doors of the mausoleum sprang open. Light flooded in. Jack's eyes, once they had adjusted to the brightness, looked at the frieze once again. The stone figure was, without a doubt, lifeless, such that Jack felt confident enough to prod it. It now felt cold, and yet, on its teeth, was that not blood he could see?

Jack tarried no longer. He scurried out into the sunshine in search of other living beings – even Mr Tumbler's presence would have been welcome! To his surprise, though, the place was deserted: no people, no carriages, nothing. He had been abandoned.

Jack sat on the rocks a while. From his breast pocket, he pulled out a white, folded handkerchief – the final accessory provided by the tailor – and spent some time fastening it round his injured wrist. He didn't want blood on his new suit.

As he sat there, basking on a rocky outcrop in the sunshine, he began to feel drowsy and soon fell into a doze. Almost immediately, he began to dream. He dreamt he was back in the mausoleum, trapped within the frieze, vainly struggling to pull himself free. But the more he struggled, the tighter the stone seemed to hold him, until he could scarcely move at all. He woke in a sweat, to find he'd slipped between two boulders. Back in the land of the living, he relaxed and soon freed himself.

Looking back towards the mausoleum, he could see that the doors were now shut. Had it all been a bad dream, he wondered. But a throbbing at his wrist made him realise it had not. After another few minutes, lying in the sun, recollecting the morning's strange events, he realised that he had little option but to make his own way back to Verona.

Stumbling along the hot dusty track, he reflected on the irony of his situation. He might have just inherited a fortune, yet here he was, tramping the countryside like a beggar. Certainly, Mr Tumbler had told him nothing about his current situation, or explained why he'd gone off without saying a word to his client. Why had Mr Cumbersome abandoned him?

As he continued on his way back to Verona, he came to the conclusion that he was not cut out for this sort of life. Delivering messages had been a far simpler existence. However, just as he was beginning to feel completely forsaken, an oxcart pulled alongside him and, through sign language, Jack realised he was being offered a ride. The man took him all the way to the city gate, restoring Jack's faith in humanity. "Grazie, grazie," intoned Jack, embarrassed that he could not say more.

Somehow, he found his way from the gate to his hotel. He took himself straight to his room and, after discarding his suit, collapsed into bed. Once again, he found himself dreaming that he was trapped within the frieze. This time, when he woke, he found that he'd managed to twist himself within his bedclothes. His wrist was again throbbing.

Jack got up and took a bath (a rare treat) before changing into some fresh clothes and going down to the lobby. Here, someone caught sight of his wrist and insisted on dressing it properly. Another member of staff then passed Jack a note. He was delighted to see that it was from Mr Cumbersome, asking Jack to meet him at a nearby taverna at six o'clock, which was just half-an-hour away. Jack asked directions and set off for their rendezvous.

He found Mr Cumbersome hidden away in an alcove. "My dear fellow, I feared the worst," he said, greeting Jack like a long-lost friend. He indicated the seat opposite and poured Jack a glass of wine. "Oh, and your wrist! What have you done?"

Jack dismissed the wound as a mere scratch from scuffing the mausoleum stonework.

"I cannot apologise enough for this morning's events," continued Cumbersome. "Abandoning you like that! You must think me very rude."

"It certainly wasn't *you* who abandoned me," said Jack, with some passion.

"And where did you get to?" enquired Cumbersome. "My partner said you'd disappeared. He thought you'd returned with the others."

Jack bridled at this, becoming quite tearful as he told Cumbersome how he'd been left at the mausoleum, but he omitted any mention of his spooky encounter. Cumbersome was particularly surprised to hear that Jack knew nothing about his inheritance. So, when Jack was informed that he was to receive £150 immediately, he was all smiles. For an errand boy, it sounded a fortune.

They then paused while some antipasti were ordered: salami, mortadella, prosciutto, bread, cheese and olives. Only when they were into their second glass of wine did Cumbersome elaborate on events. The rest of the inheritance, he explained to Jack, might now go to Alfonso Giuliani, the legitimate heir, who had suddenly reappeared.

"When Mr Tumbler returned earlier today, I initially thought it was *you* sitting with him, but … it was not. It was Alfonso."

"Well, that's alright," said Jack. "With £150, I can still get myself a barrow and sell fruit and stuff. I'll be set up."

Cumbersome smiled indulgently. "Are you a Bible reader, Jack?" he asked. The lad shrugged. "Deuteronomy 5," went on the solicitor: "'For I, the Lord your God, am a jealous God, visiting the iniquity of the fathers on the children, and on the third and the fourth generations.' Ever heard that before?" Jack nodded, recalling Sunday school. "Well, Mr Alfonso is, indeed, of the fourth generation."

"Fourth generation since what?"

"Since your great-grandfather, Arturo Carmello, was murdered by the Giuliani family."

"Murdered!"

"Unfortunately so. The Giulianis were not an honourable lot. The reason they approached an

English firm to oversee their affairs was to avoid the scrutiny of their countrymen."

Mr Cumbersome paused as the food appeared. For a while, they ate in silence, Jack scrupulously following Cumbersome's culinary example. Eventually, the lawyer poured more wine and continued.

"The Giulianis were part of an unpleasant cult that sought to purify the race. I don't really understand much of it, but the long and the short is, your great-grandfather was sacrificed in some primitive ritual."

Jack almost choked.

"At first, the Giuliani family pretended your ancestor had met with an accident. But then their misfortunes began. The firstborn sons of the next two generations died before reaching their majority. The son was killed when his 'spooked' horse crushed him. As for the grandson, he was out on a wild boar hunt and somehow managed to fall from a rocky ledge, although he knew the terrain well. Both suffered similar, fatal injuries: multiple broken bones. The grandson was just ten at the time."

Again, Cumbersome took a breather while they finished their antipasti, washed down with yet more wine.

"Old Giuliani, who survived this carnage, was devastated. After the initial death of his son under his horse, the old man attempted to divert the curse by encouraging a liaison between his nephew and your paternal grandmother. But then, when your father – the *bastardo* in question – grew up in rude health, the old count was incensed. And, of course, he dared not harm any more Carmellos! So, he paid to be rid of them, securing their emigration to England. He perhaps thought that a good deed might appease the curse.

"It did not. Only one of the dead grandson's sisters produced a boy and he, too, never reached adulthood. A bizarre fall from the roof of the family villa finished him. We then come to the fourth generation, with Alfonso's birth. He was the only child of Count Giuliani's granddaughter, who died giving birth to him. From day one, Alfonso was swaddled in cotton wool."

Cumbersome reached for the recently delivered coffee pot and poured for the two of them. "Which brings me to your involvement." He looked sharply at Jack. "When the Giulianis heard about your father's death, their hopes were raised. Perhaps, after all, the curse *had* been passed on (though your father was almost fifty at the time!). So, with the death of Alfonso's great aunt, the old count's sister, it was agreed that the young man would go into hiding, and you would be summoned."

"You mean," Jack stirred in his chair, "if there was to be a fourth-generation victim, they hoped it would be me?"

Cumbersome nodded. "I'd like to emphasise that I had no knowledge of this plan until my colleague, Mr Tumbler, enlightened me."

Eventually, they walked back to the hotel, the lawyer protectively taking Jack by the arm. Jack went immediately to bed, still worn out after the day's events.

He enjoyed several hours sleep before something woke him. He wasn't sure what. At first, he thought it was his wrist, now throbbing painfully. But then he heard banging overhead. Someone seemed to be slinging furniture around. Was it a domestic row? Jack wondered. Then, after a final, climactic clatter, silence resumed. The throbbing in his wrist also ceased and, once again, Jack fell into a slumber.

The next morning, Jack was coming out of the lift when Mr Tumbler pushed by him without a word. The lawyer was followed by a porter, laden with luggage, scurrying after him. They both left the hotel as the police entered.

Now that Jack looked around, he could see that the whole hotel was in disarray with staff appearing distracted. The breakfast room was in similar turmoil. However, Jack was pleased to see Mr Cumbersome looking as unflustered as ever.

"I just saw Mr Tumbler leave the hotel," began Jack.

"Your last sight of him, I suspect," said Cumbersome. "Do have some breakfast, then I suggest we go somewhere quieter."

They ate in companionable silence while the waiters moved uneasily around the tables. As Cumbersome had suggested, they then relocated to their previous rendezvous, the taverna. Once settled, they ordered coffee and Cumbersome updated Jack, revealing some information that he, himself, had only recently gleaned.

According to Tumbler, the plan had been for Alfonso to lie low, protecting himself – as they'd already discussed. But the boy had been too eager to pursue his inheritance, which was why Tumbler had so suddenly raced over from England, to keep him out of the limelight. Alfonso, though – a hot-headed youth – had been unable to resist going to the mausoleum. "Tumbler had brought him back, as you know, and hidden him in the hotel."

"Alfonso was there?"

"*Was* is the right word," said Cumbersome. "Brace yourself, my boy. The curse has finally claimed its fourth-generation victim. Alfonso Giuliani is dead."

Jack almost dropped his coffee cup.

"He was found this morning, his body – bizarrely – exhibiting the same signs of morbidity as his ancestors'. That is, a number of bones had been broken, as if he'd been crushed by something – a horse, possibly – or fallen from a great height." Cumbersome poured more coffee. "Except that, he can only have fallen out of bed!"

Jack recalled the bangs and bumps he'd heard, then Mr Tumbler's hasty departure, the strange behaviour of the hotel staff, the arrival of the police. It all now fitted together, although Jack would like to have dismissed his thoughts as fanciful. It really was like one of his penny dreadful serials. However, the memory of that leering stone figure cleaved his tongue. Somehow, Jack was convinced, that creature was responsible for

Alfonso's death and, perhaps, the deaths of others, too. Would it now come looking for him?

With this thought, Jack managed to siphon his last mouthful of coffee down his nose and started to choke.

"O my goodness!" Cumbersome was on his feet, slapping Jack on the back. "Don't croak on us now, old chap!"

When the two returned to the hotel, the police were still there. Although Jack could hardly have been capable of causing Alfonso's injuries, the authorities were duty-bound to interview him, given that he might now be the main beneficiary of the Giuliani estate, with a vested interest in Alfonso's demise.

The interview was an ordeal, especially as it had to be conducted through an interpreter (fortunately, Cumbersome obliged). But Jack found it less intimidating than what he was asked to do afterwards, for the police had tracked down the man who had driven Alfonso to the mausoleum (in the carriage that Jack had thought he'd heard).

Accordingly, the driver, along with Jack, the priest, and some of the others present at the mausoleum, had been requested to attend a reconstruction of the events leading to Alfonso's bizarre death. The police had really wanted Mr Tumbler there, but he, of course, was unavailable.

Eventually, the moment came when Jack was asked to re-enact his time alone in the mausoleum. He was panicky. They were asking him to replay his worst nightmare! However, he soon realised it would not be as before, for not only would the chief of police have to be present but, because of the language barrier, Mr Cumbersome too. Aside from that, the whole interior now looked different, ablaze with candlelight.

Standing in front of the frieze, Jack tried to show them how he had cut his wrist on the stone figure's teeth, except that this action proved impossible, for the teeth curved inward. Jack realised he was making little sense. Fortunately, Mr Cumbersome seemed to be conveying a more convincing story to the police chief, who nodded appreciatively.

While they talked, Jack summoned the courage to look more directly at the sneering figure. But the sneer had gone. Jack smiled as it dawned on him what the figure had really been doing yesterday. It had been establishing his blood line and discovered, presumably, that he was not related to the Giulianis after all. That, Jack surmised, must have been a rumour spread by the family in order to outwit the curse. But the curse knew better – and it had now run its course … or so Jack hoped.

Needless to say, Jack shared none of these thoughts with the police, nor with Mr Cumbersome. He looked again at the stone figure. It would be fanciful to say that they exchanged a look, but somehow, Jack felt he had a confidant. The sneer now looked almost like a grin.

2

On the journey back to London, Mr Cumbersome had made Jack consider his future carefully, advising him that, when his inheritance was finalised, he should acquire some property, investing his capital in something solid and worthwhile. He might, for example, consider buying a new house for his family.

However, as Jack had anticipated, his mother refused to leave the East End. She was quite happy, she said, living where she was, together with some Russian refugees they'd recently taken in.

Cumbersome had also suggested that Jack buy a place for himself and, of course, give up being an errand boy. Jack, though, couldn't contemplate being on his own – especially after his recent experiences. He was quite content, he told Cumbersome, to stay on at Mrs Jade's, even if he wasn't running errands all day.

In the event, though, Jack found his new life very strange and unsatisfactory. He would still join his pals for the morning rush, getting up at 6.30 and poking down his breakfast with them. However, they'd then scurry off to work, leaving him at a loss. He would wander the capital, supposedly exploring London's sights (another suggestion of Mr Cumbersome's). More often than not, though, Jack would end up in a teashop drinking endless cuppas. In the evenings, he'd re-join his pals for an evening meal and listen enviously to the day's events.

Jack was obviously mindful that his friends knew about his elevated status. He tried his best to share his good fortune with them, funding outings – like a trip to the new picture palace and treating the lads to gobstoppers, wine gums and fizzy pop. But a gulf was opening between them, as Jack was well aware. Cumbersome had been right: it had been a mistake trying to hold on to his old life. Even with his best friend Bob, some of the magic had gone.

❈

Three weeks after Jack's return, a small package was delivered to Mrs Jade's, all the way from Italy. The lads had gone off to work, so she was the only one to see Jack open it. Inside the brown paper and corrugated cardboard, Jack uncovered a small box and a letter. He opened the latter and read it through, pleased with his new accomplishment of reading silently. The letter, dated 3rd June 1910, was from Mr Tumbler, someone Jack had never expected to hear from again.

The lawyer expressed his regrets at the way events had unfolded. It was, he said, beyond his control. He also apologised for the length of time it was taking to sort out Jack's inheritance. But, as the lawyer explained, there were many interested parties involved in the estate. However, as Tumbler went on, given that he was also responsible for sorting out Alfonso Giuliani's affairs, he could pass on the Giuliani ring, which was traditionally worn by the next eligible male relative.

Jack was honoured, though surprised to receive this news from Tumbler rather than Cumbersome. Jack opened the box and gazed at the heavy gold ring with a crest on the top.

"That's some lump of ring!" exclaimed Mrs Jade.

Jack's initial reaction, though, was one of revulsion. He really didn't want anything more to do with that despicable family, regardless of how well off they might eventually make him. They had, after all, murdered his grandfather. He decided, therefore, to put the thing away.

However, as he made his way upstairs, he slipped the ring onto his finger, just to see how it looked. It was certainly impressive and fitted him perfectly. Standing before the bedroom mirror, he felt an inward glow. What a toff he was becoming!

❀

Mr Cumbersome was certainly surprised to hear Jack's news. Having heard nothing since his partner's hasty departure, Cumbersome presumed the man had been incarcerated by the Italian authorities. Certainly, as Cumbersome frequently complained, Tumbler's disappearance had burdened him with a great deal of extra work.

After admiring the ring, Cumbersome showed Jack how it functioned. He melted some wax in a metal container then dropped a blob of the hot liquid onto some paper before getting Jack to imprint the crest of the ring in the solidifying wax. Jack was impressed. There was the Giuliani crest: twin greyhounds, head to toe, between which stood a bundle of sticks wrapped around an axe head.

"It's a signet ring – allowing you to leave your official signet-ure," said Cumbersome, smiling at his wordplay. "However, it is easier to use such a ring when it's worn on the little finger," he added.

Jack swapped it immediately, and both were surprised to see how well it seemed to adapt to the smaller digit. But more surprising to Jack was the feeling he'd experienced as the ring changed fingers. The ring resisted its initial removal. And, when Jack finally tugged it free, he felt strangely bereft until the ring was snug on his little finger.

That evening, Jack showed the ring to the others. "Proper count now, aren't we?" said Tom, a relative newcomer to Mrs Jade's. Jack thought the lad was a bit out of order, especially given the way he mispronounced count, but Jack said nothing. He was relieved when it was time for bed and he and Bob bade the others goodnight.

"'*Bunny hoppy*'?" queried Bob as they climbed the stairs. Jack looked perplexed. "That foreign stuff you was spouting at them," clarified Bob.

"*Buona notte*?" Jack suggested. "Did I say that?"

"Right little Eyetalian you're becoming," said Bob, "and you don't even know it!"

In the morning, he and Bob managed to bag the bathroom first. They stood alongside each other, shaving. Neither really needed to, but it was a marker of manhood that each was keen to cultivate.

Jack had had a particularly disturbing night, the stone figure – a not infrequent nocturnal visitor – pervading his dreams. So perhaps he wasn't concentrating enough, for his razor suddenly skidded over his cheek and down across his outstretched throat. Despite swiftly arresting the blade's momentum, Jack still managed to nick his flesh.

Bob took a step back. "Cor! Not called a cutthroat for nothing," he joked.

Jack, dripping blood, tried to staunch the flow with cold water and soap. The two watched as the lather in the bowl turned from pink to a deeper red. At this point, Jack made the mistake of looking his reflection in the eye. His cutthroat clattered into the basin, splashing Bob.

"Blimey, Jack! You's a clumsy article today!"

"*Scusi*," Jack muttered.

"You what?" said Bob. He flicked the lather off his own cutthroat, splattering Jack's reflection in the mirror. "You don't even know you're doing it, do you?" said Bob, this time flicking the residue of lather directly at Jack. "Anyway," said Bob, making his way out the door, "Some of us 'as work to go to!"

❨✺❩

Jack said hardly anything during breakfast. He watched enviously as his pals bustled around before heading off on their daily errands. Life had been so simple until recently: go here, deliver this; go there, deliver that. Now he felt rudderless.

He returned to his room and put on his jacket, hat and the new ring. After Tom's comment the night before, he'd resisted wearing it at breakfast, though it had proved a struggle.

Outside, it was sunny and warm – more like Verona weather, in fact – and Jack immediately felt better. He wandered idly – something he did most days – and soon found himself in Hyde Park. Following the crowds, he ended up at Speakers' Corner.

It was providential. The speaker seemed to be addressing Jack's personal concerns directly. According to him – Mr Mancaster, a posh-sounding man in a check suit, sporting a fine pair of moustaches – an increasing number of English people felt displaced, as though they didn't belong anymore. Thanks to a foreign invasion, English customs and values were being lost, with immigrants stealing Englishmen's jobs.

"England for the English!" went up the cry, and Jack was soon chanting alongside the others in the swelling audience.

After the meeting, many in the crowd made their way to the East End. Jack tagged along. When they came across a street market, some of the lads started upsetting the stacked goods on the stalls and pinching items. A woman who challenged them had her cart overturned. They ran off, laughing. Jack realised he also needed to run, or risk arrest. As he charged down the street with them, he pictured himself as Spring-heeled Jack, the penny dreadful hero. It was a name that Bob sometimes conferred on him. Jack felt energised, his blood pounding through him.

When the police appeared, the lads scattered. Jack, most familiar with the neighbourhood, led the way. They were quite near his parents' house. He had thought of hiding there with a few of his new acquaintances, but then remembered his grandparents, who still looked and sounded Italian; and then there were the Russian immigrants! Jack led them elsewhere, quickly outpacing their flatfooted pursuers.

❀

Over time, Jack became more involved with this rebellious bunch, known as The Brotherhood. At first, he'd tried to conceal his Italian background, but one day, while they were in a bar listening to Mancaster speak, Jack had let slip the provenance of his ring. He knew he shouldn't wear such a valuable thing so openly, but he couldn't bear to take it off.

To Jack's surprise, Mr Mancaster expressed a respect for Italy's "rediscovery of its glorious Roman past. Even now, it is seeking to recover its historical territories through a policy of irridentism." Although Jack was not sure what irridentism meant, he began to view his Italian heritage more positively. Before long, he realised he actually thought of himself as a Giuliani, not a Carmello, despite the fact that, if he had been one of them, the curse would have exterminated him by now. Once again, Jack recalled the granular hold of that stone figure, and shuddered.

It was only a few days after this that "Jacko", as he now liked to be known, received another communication from Mr Tumbler. The man apologised for the delay in finalising the conditions of the will: tying up loose ends, unpicking the intricacies of tenancies and leaseholds, establishing ownership and stewardship of the various farms, vineyards and other properties. Jack had heard Mr Cumbersome say similar things, although there were hints that he held his partner responsible for the delays.

However, Tumbler's letter did suggest a way forward, given that Jack's legitimacy (or official status as *bastardo*) was one of the main bones of contention. Tumbler recommended that Jack appear in Verona in person. As he read these words, Jack's face lit up. It was as though some unconscious plan he'd been formulating was finally coming to fruition. Bizarrely, Jack saw it in terms of returning to his homeland.

The letter concluded by requesting a swift response from Jack, while cautioning him – "at the risk of jeopardising your inheritance" – against sharing this plan with Cumbersome. Jack was shocked. That man was his mentor, the one who'd seen him through so many scrapes. Even now, though they disagreed on many things (like Jack's association with The Brotherhood), Mr Cumbersome – unlike Tumbler – was his ally. This said, the opportunity to return to Italy burned in Jack's mind such that it soon overrode all other considerations. Besides which, Jack thought he might be able to slip away and return without Cumbersome even noticing his absence.

Jack thus accepted Tumbler's invitation and, shortly thereafter, tickets and other official documents were couriered to him. As he received the documents from the errand boy, Jack found himself chuckling. Only a short while ago, he would have been the courier. He tipped the boy generously.

❦❀❦

This trip to Verona formed a marked contrast to his last one. Jack felt so much more confident. The idea that he was going back to the fatherland – rather than leaving it behind – had lodged itself in his mind. And the closer he came to Verona, with its distinctive landscape, smells and sounds, the stronger grew this notion of homecoming. The stronger, too, grew Jack's command of Italian, which had previously been rudimentary.

Jack didn't expect Tumbler to meet him at the train station and, sure enough, the man was nowhere to be seen. Before long, though, Jack was approached by a man with a cart who had been sent to escort Jack to the hotel. Jack was buoyant at his ability to journey across Europe on his own. However, as the Stazione di Verona hotel loomed ahead, his confidence waned.

The hideous sounds of Alfonso's murder suddenly rang in his head. Moreover, although it had all taken place in the room above him, the memory was so visceral that Jack pictured himself experiencing the crushing grip of the stone figure, his bruised bones finally cracking and splintering, his lungs puncturing and then … that awful choking sensation as the blood bubbled in his windpipe.

"Hey!" shouted a voice. It released Jack from that dreadful memory. The driver, he realised, was shouting at him for, unwittingly, Jack had hold of his arm. As Jack once again took in his surroundings, he saw that they had now moved beyond the Stazione to their destination. Jack let out the breath he'd been holding. He was a Carmello, he reassured himself, not a Giuliani. Hence, he was still alive.

As Jack checked in, he was handed a note from Tumbler. It suggested a meeting the following morning, at eleven, on the hotel terrace.

Exhausted, Jack unpacked his essentials and, although it was still early, readied himself for bed. Brushing his teeth in front of the small mirror beside his jug and ewer, though, Jack had another disturbing experience. His features suddenly appeared alien. His lips looked fuller, redder; his nose more prominent and aquiline; his brows thicker and his complexion darker, showing the distinct shadow of stubble. In another second, his face was back to normal, apart from his gaping mouth, out of which the white tooth powder drooled.

Ever since that earlier experience with the cutthroat razor, Jack had been wary of mirrors, but he tried not to dwell on that now. "I need some rest!" he told himself, not even noticing that he'd said it in Italian.

Unfortunately, his dreams offered little respite, The stone man was there again, lying across Jack's chest, suffocating him. Jack had tried in vain to throw him off. After what seemed an age, he finally woke, gasping for air. As he became more conscious of his surroundings, he realised that he was lying, *not* on his back, but on his chest. The immoveable object against which he had been pushing so fruitlessly, was the mattress beneath him.

Jack gave up on sleep. It was now early morning. He dressed and went out for some fresh air. Despite everything, he loved Verona and, in this pale, early morning light, it looked spectacular. Apart from a few road cleaners, he encountered no one until he came across a group of young men performing gymnastics in a park. Jack stopped to admire their muscular, tanned bodies before eventually returning to the hotel for breakfast.

After that, he sat on the terrace, nursing a coffee, awaiting Tumbler. He hardly recognised the man who finally approached him, though, for he had changed so much. Tumbler had been a big man before, but he was now heavier than ever. But Jack also thought the man looked less formidable, perhaps because Jack was conscious of his flakiness.

"Good to see you again, er, Jack. Or, perhaps, Giacomo?" he said, extending his hand.

Jack took it, surprised both at the man's unexpected civility and the fact that he'd used the Italian version of his name. Jack didn't object. He already thought of himself as "Jacko."

"And this is Signor Ludovico Bianchi," said Tumbler, turning to the gentleman alongside him. This had been another reason why Jack didn't recognise the lawyer. He'd been looking for someone on his own. "Signor Bianchi was keen to meet a representative of the Giuliani family," said Tumbler, gesturing to the empty seats. "May we?"

Jack nodded and started to explain that he was not a proper Giuliani. However, they were not listening, busy calling over the waiter.

Bianchi was an impressive figure: taller than most Italians and with pale skin. He wore a fedora hat, perhaps to protect his clean-shaven skin. Jack put the man in his mid-thirties.

Bianchi's agenda dominated the conversation, with no mention of a meeting with the Giulianis. Bianchi,

Jack gathered, was a politician of sorts, who intended to hold a rally in the Arena di Verona – a well-preserved Roman amphitheatre in the city – to launch a new political movement, one that recognised Italy as the obvious place to found a new Roman Empire.

Bianchi said he was very keen that the Giulianis – the greatest and oldest family in Venetia – were officially represented. Once again, Jack started to protest but Tumbler spoke over him.

"Giacomo," he said, "we think it would be wise if you used the Giuliani name while you are here, making your position more official."

Jack had no objection. In fact, he delighted in the idea, knowing that it would help secure his position as rightful heir, while he was also aware that he was immune to the Giuliani curse. Bianchi then gestured to a gang of youths on the far side of the terrace. They were the group Jack had admired earlier, practising their gymnastics.

"Some outstanding examples of our new Italian youth," proclaimed Bianchi, idly reaching out an arm and squeezing the bicep of the youth nearest him. "Along with others, they will give an impressive display of Italian strength and discipline in the Arena." Bianchi reached out to another of his acolytes, massaging the young man's shoulder.

Jack was surprised when Bianchi then reached over and took Jack by the arm. His grip was disturbingly reminiscent of the stone man's. "This is Giacomo

Giuliani," announced Bianchi, holding up Jack's arm and pointing to the ring on his little finger. "The oldest son of our most celebrated family."

Bianchi proceeded to explain the symbolism of the bundle of sticks encompassing the axe head. "The fasces represent unity, strength in numbers and singleness of purpose. But also," and here he indicated the protruding axe, "might and power." Letting go of Jack's arm, Bianchi interlaced his own hands and executed a scything sweep with his arms extended. He was imitating the grim reaper, of course, but in Jack's mind, the reaper was a man of stone.

Until this moment, Jack had not been sure why Bianchi had spent so long describing the fasces, but he now witnessed each member of the troupe flexing his right bicep, shirtsleeves rolled tight to display their tattoo of that symbol.

Bianchi turned again to Jack. "We are so pleased to have the blessing of the Giuliani family," he said.

Jack was not sure what was being agreed to. Permission to use the fasces symbol, or the family name? Or … did they expect Jack to donate some of his inheritance? For the moment, he just nodded approvingly.

Nico, who seemed to be the leader of the troupe, now turned to Jack, inviting him to watch them perform in the Piazza dei Signori that evening. Jack was honoured, despite being acutely conscious of how weedy a specimen he looked alongside them. Clearly, it was the Giuliani name that carried the kudos. Jack looked to Mr Tumbler, in case the lawyer had any alternative plans, but the man was ignoring him, talking animatedly to Bianchi. Jack told Nico he'd be delighted to attend.

€🎇Э

It turned out to be a most eventful evening. Nico and his team demonstrated not only their gymnastic proficiency but also their skills in acrobatics, swordsmanship, boxing and juggling. After their performance, when the crowds had dispersed, Nico suggested a few drinks. Jack was game.

Being out with the lads reminded him of nights with The Brotherhood. Both groups enjoyed a drink, a joke – and a fight or two. But, after a few glasses of wine, Jack knew he'd had enough. He excused himself, thanking them for their companionship and – only at that moment – realising that all evening he'd been speaking Italian.

Heading back to his hotel, Jack became aware of feet thumping behind him. Initially, he thought it must be Bianchi's boys, keen to prolong the night's fun. But, as Jack turned, a fist cracked him on the temple. It was a gang of street urchins, dressed in ragged clothing, some even barefoot. What they lacked in attire, though, they made up for in weaponry. They brandished slings, catapults, sticks and knives.

Jack was wondering why he'd been picked on. He didn't look particularly affluent. But next thing, he felt someone tugging at his hand. Of course! His ring. It always attracted attention. Jack was about to put up some resistance when he saw a blade in his attacker's hand. He was going to lose his finger! Jack quickly tugged off the ring, flinging it down the street. As it rang over the cobbles, he felt an immediate pang of loss. Even so, his finger was far more precious.

The only other thing he could do was yell. "*Ladro!*" he attempted to say, but the word was suddenly meaningless. "Thief!" was all he could enunciate.

He had hoped Bianchi's boys would hear him, but it was someone else who responded. Amidst the street urchins who were fighting amongst themselves for possession of the ring, another figure materialised. Suddenly, the boys in the midst of the fray were laid waste like ninepins. Jack was momentarily confused: was it the cavalry, or was it his Calvary? For there stood the stone man, whose bottomless eye sockets seemed to swallow him, and, indeed, almost everything else in the Piazza. Jack was therefore oblivious to the Bianchi Boys charging into view, pursuing the remaining street kids down passageways. Only Nico and one other stayed behind to attend to Jack.

"What did they do to you, Giacomo?" Nico was saying, but Jack couldn't understand a word. All he managed to do was waggle his little finger, showing the lighter skin where the Giuliani band no longer shone.

The Bianchi Boys carried Jack back to his hotel, making sure he was safe in his room before leaving him. Jack lay on his bed, confused. What was going on? What was he doing here? He now felt a desperate yearning to be back, safe and sound, in England. To be back with Cumbersome, Bob, his Mum, the lads …

❧✸☙

It was late morning before a maid discovered Jack in his room. She thought the broken young man, sprawled across the bed, was a corpse. She informed the manager, who summoned Tumbler, his name gleaned from a booking slip.

Tumbler arrived, but only for a brief reconnaissance. Seeing Jack lying there, Tumbler experienced an awful sense of déjà vu, recalling his earlier discovery of Alfonso's body, crushed and misshapen. Back then, Tumbler had gone to Alfonso's room to discuss some legal matters, but when he'd beheld the state of play, he'd thought it wise to take charge of the Giuliani ring. However, it turned out to be a harder task than he'd envisaged, for the ring had become embedded in Alfonso's flesh. Tumbler had taken the view that more damage to the body would make little difference. He had twisted the finger until, with a snap, both finger and ring were freed.

Looking down at Jack, though, Tumbler could see that, this time, there was no ring. Once again, as he now realised, his plans had been thwarted. Ringless, and in this condition, Jack would be of no use to Bianchi's cause, which meant that Tumbler would, once again, have to disappear.

Before he left, though, Tumbler undertook two uncharacteristic actions. He arranged for Jack to be conveyed to hospital and then contacted the London office of the firm that still bore his name, requesting that his partner be informed of Jack's condition and whereabouts. Cumbersome, he knew, was good at this sort of thing.

☾❋☽

Less than a week later, a shocked Cumbersome appeared at the Sisters of Mercy Hospital, whence Jack had been removed. The lawyer felt partly responsible for Jack's condition and, over the next few days, spent many hours at his bedside. However, as Jack showed no signs of reviving from his trance-like state, Cumbersome eventually acquiesced to the procedure recommended by the sisters: an exorcism.

Over the next five days, the Prayer for St Michael was recited. However, nothing dramatic resulted. Had this purgation begun earlier, when Jack was still under Alfonso's spell, things might been different. But Giuliani's malevolent presence had departed with the ring. All that the hospital bed contained was Jack's bodily shell. His spirit was elsewhere, carried off by the stone man. When Jack, lying comatose, had seen that figure approaching, he'd anticipated some crushing blows, but they were not forthcoming. The creature simply carried him away, doors and walls proving no obstacle.

It was only as they journeyed out of Verona that the identity of this stone man finally dawned on Jack. It was his great-grandfather, Arturo Carmello, the man murdered by the Giulianis.

Up into the hills, the figure took Jack and, before he knew it, he once again found himself in that fearful mausoleum, except that this time Jack felt safe and secure, alongside Arturo, suspended within the frieze.

☾✺☽

Back at the Sisters of Mercy Hospital, Cumbersome gazed down at Jack's inert form, not sure what more could be done. The only time that Jack had shown any signs of life was when Cumbersome had addressed him directly. But Cumbersome realised he was not close enough to Jack. That's when he recalled the boy talking about his best friend, Bob.

It was a long shot, but Cumbersome took immediate action. Jack was too ill to travel, so Bob would have to come to Verona. The lawyer arranged for one of the practice's scriveners to accompany him. As Cumbersome also needed someone to courier across documentation relating to the Giuliani estate, this suited him well (he realised he would get nothing out of Tumbler).

Eventually, an awestruck Bob arrived and Cumbersome escorted him to Jack's bedside. Bob hardly recognised the wasted figure. Jack's skin had the feel of builders' sand. Nevertheless, Bob did as he'd been bidden, chattering away to Jack about old times: their japes at Mrs Jade's, their journeys to and fro across London, delivering and collecting packages.

It was the tonic Jack needed. After several hours of Bob's unrelenting chat, Jack felt some part of himself detach from the frieze and come back to him. Shortly thereafter, the hospitalised Jack opened his eyes. "Are you never going to shut up?" he muttered through parched lips. "We need some shut-eye before morning!"

Bob grinned.

After this, Jack's recovery was dramatic. Cumbersome, freed from Jack's bedside, had managed to make some progress on the Giuliani estate and all three of them – Jack, Bob and Cumbersome – planned to return to London. Jack, however, announced that he had one more thing to do.

Cumbersome feared that it might involve attending the imminent Bianchi rally at the Arena, so was relieved when he heard Jack dismiss Bianchi and those "crazy irredentists". To Bob, it sounded as though Jack were speaking Eyetie again. His friend pictured a mob of angry dentists. It was a line that would later become a standing joke between the pals.

"I need to visit the Giuliani mausoleum," said Jack. Cumbersome was nonplussed but readily agreed.

❄

Jack appeared surprisingly calm as the three of them entered the vault, each bearing a candle. Mr Cumbersome watched Jack march resolutely towards the frieze. All of a sudden, he halted in shock. Ahead of him, on a raised platform next to the great aunt, was the casket of the most recent Giuliani casualty: Alfonso. It was the more shocking for being such a small container, clearly all that was needed for Alfonso's crushed remains. Cumbersome was about to offer Jack some support when he heard the lad mutter, "*Scusi.*"

Jack moved across to the frieze.

He said only one other word before they all left the mausoleum: "Arturo."

Bob and Cumbersome watched in awe as Jack reached out to the stone figure. It must have been a trick of the light for, as Jack ran his hand over the carved features, they seemed to respond to his touch. His lawyer also watched Jack trace the faint outline of something alongside the stone man, some inchoate figure that the stonemason seemed to have abandoned.

❄

Back in London, all three were in good spirits. Jack, in particular, looked more his old self. Cumbersome had bought a newspaper which carried a report on Bianchi's rally. "New Italian Renaissance dawns?" it queried. "Irredentist cause gains momentum."

What the newspaper did not mention was that an impressionable young man named Benito Mussolini had been there and, somehow, had come into possession of the Giuliani ring. At the time, it meant little, but, down the years, the consequences would be seismic for both Jack and Bob, alongside millions of others.

That was the future, though.

For the present, Jack looked forward to seeing his proper family once again, and rejoicing in the anonymity of Mrs Jade's boarding house, where he intended to resume his career as an errand boy. Of course, before he broke this news to Mr Cumbersome, he would choose his moment carefully.

Lithe Spirit

First-class train travel was going to be a treat for Catherine, or so she had thought. Never before had she "indulged" herself, as she put it, but this was a special occasion. She was off to London to see her sister, Doris, the day before her sibling's sixtieth birthday, which was on Wednesday 14th February. So, when Catherine had been offered a last-minute upgrade, she took it, also treating herself to a new travel bag, a dark-beige trouser suit and a pale-yellow

.blouse. At this rate, thought Catherine, Doris wouldn't recognise her.

On the journey itself, Catherine had worked hard at making herself comfortable but, somehow, she couldn't find a position in which she felt relaxed. It was ridiculous, she thought. Everyone else seemed to be at their ease, luxuriating in the extra legroom.

She'd thrown down her magazine in disgust. It was then that she'd smelled the aroma of fresh coffee. That was what was missing, she'd decided. On cue, a smart young steward had proffered her a cup – a proper china cup, too (not one of those awful cardboard things) – and presented her with a selection of biscuits. She'd removed her jacket and hung it up. "This is more like it," she'd reassured herself. Except that it wasn't.

Having finished the coffee, Catherine thought she'd located the problem: a cold draught at her back. Though no one else seemed to be suffering from it, she was sure it wasn't her imagination. Thoughtfully, an attendant had turned up the heating for her, but that only made her skin prickle. Next, she'd requested a blanket, aware that the label "problem passenger" must now be prominent against seat C-03. The blanket made no difference either.

As she went to use the toilet, Catherine was aware she'd left the coldness behind. It was, indeed, a draught local to C-03, for elsewhere on the train, she experienced no discomfort at all. Had first class not been full, she would have asked to change seats. As it was, she ended up sitting in the non-exclusive buffet car for the greater part of the journey, foregoing the complimentary refreshments and personalised service that, so untypically, she'd paid for.

❆

Tom only travelled once a year, to attend his annual school reunion, and always went first class. In fact, he always tried to reserve his favourite seat: "number three in carriage C". Since 1957, when he'd become an "old boy" of St Paul's in London, he'd hardly missed a year, apart from when his wife had been terminally ill. It now seemed more important than ever to be present, given how few of his contemporaries were still around. He always found it a shock when "Absent Friends" were toasted, each name being read out with a hiatus between, as though it were the school register being called.

This year, though, Tom's visit was to be special. Not only was there the reunion to look forward to, but his daughter, Millicent, was performing in a revival of Noel Coward's *Blithe Spirit* at the Apollo Theatre. The reunion was on Wednesday 14th February, St Valentine's Feast Day (though, as Tom had often said, "Valentine himself didn't even get to taste the starters"). Tom had therefore booked himself a seat in the stalls (L15) for the evening before, along with a Novotel room.

However, shortly before the trip, Tom was diagnosed with a tumour in his colon and emergency surgery was needed. It was feared the cancer had spread elsewhere. His consultant was circumspect, but his son, Christopher, who had been present to hear the prognosis, realised that his father needed to put his affairs in order. For a start, his London trip could not go ahead. His dad, though, had been wilfully obtuse, refusing to countenance the idea that he'd be yet another "Absent Friend", let alone missing Millicent at the Apollo theatre.

"Dad," Christopher had said, "think of it like this. Instead of the Apollo, you'll be starring in your own theatre at the Salford Royal Hospital!"

Tom had not been amused.

❈

Most of the audience at the Apollo on that Tuesday had thoroughly enjoyed the play. The exception was the occupant of seat L15, who could not understand why he had been so disenchanted. *Blithe Spirit* was one of his favourites. As a young man, Norris Clarke had himself been in amateur dramatics, and his most spectacular success had come from playing the lead: Charles Condomine, a man plagued by the ghosts of his successive wives. In fact, after his thespian triumph, Norris had been quite the VIP in his hometown. But that was over thirty years ago.

It was an old friend who'd put Norris onto this production, and who'd managed to find him a seat on a late ticket site. As Norris watched the current incumbent of the role strutting the boards – a well-known TV celebrity, so he'd been informed – Norris found himself becoming increasingly restless. "Nuance? Subtlety?" he'd wanted to shout.

He sighed. Perhaps he was being too harsh. Perhaps it wasn't the acting at all that bothered him, for he was beginning to find fault with everything. Basically, he realised, he was intensely uncomfortable. It was a feeling he'd never previously experienced in the theatre. Usually, he was so absorbed that aches and pains held off until the curtain calls.

Norris knew how distracting it was to have a restive audience, but, for the life of him, he could not sit still. He'd half-anticipated a tap on the shoulder from behind: "Excuse me, my man, could you stop squirming?" Perhaps, thought Norris, I still have a bit of Charles Condomine in me, and I'm being goosed by my spirit wives!

Before he could curb himself, he found he was chuckling aloud at this idea. Unfortunately, it was at a moment when everyone else was silent. The resentment around him was palpable. Apologising, Norris got up and left. It was the first time, ever, he'd left a play prematurely.

❈

From the other side of the proscenium arch, Millicent was perhaps the only other person who found the play an ordeal that evening. But it was understandable. Only a few hours earlier, Christopher had phoned her with news of their father's sudden death.

"He survived the operation," Christopher had informed her, "but then tried to get out of bed, tubes and all, shouting that he was off to catch a train to London – to see *you* on stage!"

That had cracked her up.

"In the end," continued Christopher, "Dad worked himself into such a state that he suffered a fatal heart attack!"

"Do you think he *could* have made it?" Millicent had asked.

"No chance," said Christopher, presuming she meant the journey, not his overall recovery. "Fortunately," he added, "I'd already cancelled the bookings."

"Right!" said Millicent, not bothering to clarify her meaning. Christopher, she knew, was always one to look after the pennies. "No point in wasting our inheritance on phantom trips!" she said, pointedly.

❈

Later that same night, Jessica had found herself at her wits' end in her Novotel room. She'd booked it late, on a whim, so that she'd be ready for her job interview on the Wednesday. Initially, she'd been going to travel up to London in the morning, but she didn't want to risk being late. This way, following a hearty breakfast, she could put on her make-up and new outfit at her leisure.

That had been the plan, but as Jessica continued to toss and turn in the early hours, she thought she might have been better staying at home. She couldn't understand it: this bed was far more comfortable than her own, and bigger. The breakfast better be good, she thought to herself.

As her clock registered 3.30 a.m., she became more convinced she'd made a mistake. Earlier in the night, she'd thought that the anonymity of the place was the problem, but she now felt the opposite. It was as though she had gate-crashed someone else's room – someone who now wanted it back. The hints were none too subtle: she kept losing the duvet and, big though the bed was, continually found herself clinging to its edge. It was as if someone, or something, were trying to elbow her out.

At 4.00 a.m. Jessica gave up. She needed to escape, she decided. Having thrown on some clothes, she stealthily exited and crept down the corridor, anxious not to disturb others.

It was strange. Almost immediately she'd left the room, she felt better, more relaxed, albeit dog tired. Spotting a comfy chair near the lifts, she collapsed into it.

❈

At the reunion on the 14th, the time came for the "Absent Friends" toast. At what would have been Tom's table, his closest friends – already alert to their school-pal's demise (thanks to his son, Christopher) – listened to the roll call. Even so, their lips trembled as they heard the name "Tom Grimsby" ring out.

But this shock was as nothing to what each thought he subsequently heard. A muted but distinctive voice breaking the deferential silence: "Present!"

Finding Closure

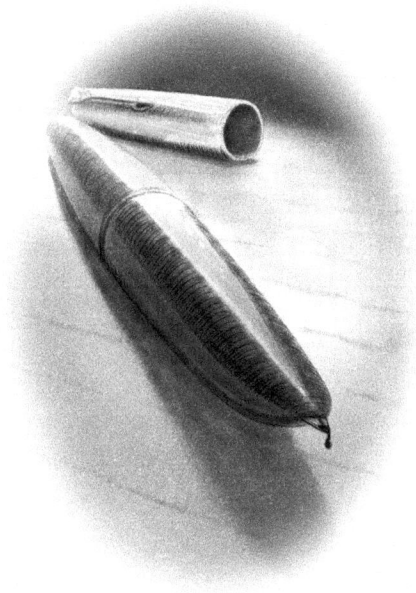

amela lay in bed listening to a scrabbling noise. It sounded as though it was coming from the walls. Since George had died, the house seemed to have turned against her. First there had been the loose roof tile, then a leak in her bedroom radiator and, finally, the electrics had started buzzing as though she had a wasps' nest somewhere.

"Oh, George," she found herself declaring, "why aren't you here when I need you?"

She eventually gave up trying to sleep. Her head was too full of disturbing memories. It was only 5.30 a.m. but she put on her nightgown and slippers and went downstairs. Each tread of the stairway seemed to creak and groan as she made her way into the hall. She turned on the kitchen light, which flickered annoyingly for several seconds as though trying to induce in her some sort of seizure.

A cup of tea and a Marmite sandwich, that's what she needed. She took them through to the lounge where she made herself comfortable on the settee. She no longer sat in her old armchair, for it stood opposite George's, where he had presided year after year: a Queen Anne wingback, with a board balanced across the arms to write those interminable letters to the press and the BBC and the Council – indeed, to anyone, really, who made a grammatical error, or misquoted, or misattributed something.

George would turn it into a test for her, too. He would present her with the newspaper, prodding a column of print with his finger. "What do you think of that?" he would ask, as she strove to find the offending error.

"Well?" came the inevitable prompt, taking Pamela back to her schooldays when her English teacher would stand over her, similarly impatient, a finger tapping her work. "What is wrong, Wright?" he would quip. Wright had been her maiden name, and how she had suffered because of it.

Sitting there now, gazing at George's chair, Pamela recalled the moment in the park when he had proposed to her and the alacrity with which she had responded, much to his surprise. Little did he know that her enthusiasm was partly prompted by the thought that she'd finally be able to escape her surname, even if it meant becoming Mrs George Higginbottom. How naïve she'd been! She smiled at the very thought as she gazed at George's empty chair.

He had been eight years older than she was and at the time she saw him as her saviour. St George rescuing her from the family home where, after her mother's untimely death from cancer, she had seen herself becoming trapped with her demanding father. He had been another man who was always right. Out of the frying pan, as her friend Betty always said.

Once again, Pamela looked across at the empty chair with George's bookcase alongside it, his reference works neatly lined up against the edge of the shelf. George had regularly checked their alignment. "Inspecting the troops," he called it.

She had always laughed at his little foibles, the way he tried to impose some sort of order on the world. Now she missed his habits; in fact, a few of them she had taken on board herself.

It had been three months now since his death. She still found herself making his morning cup of tea and placing a digestive on the saucer, and she still made sure his corner of the lounge was kept neat and tidy.

"It's like a shrine," Betty from next door had said. "Why don't you get rid?" But somehow, she hadn't been able to disturb anything associated with George.

Betty had been one of the few neighbours to attend his funeral. It was only down the road. Pamela thought a few more might have paid their respects, but she was not really surprised, for he had estranged so many of their friends with his ways.

Betty had gone with her last week, too, when she went to freshen his flowers and clean up his plot. Betty was very generous, considering that George had taken her to task for a sign she displayed in her porch: "No Junkmail, Cold Callers, Canvasers or Religious Groups."

"*Canvas* with one '*s*' is what campers sleep under," he had informed her, "whereas, to *canvass* – double '*s*' – is an activity undertaken by supporters of causes."

Pamela always giggled when she heard Betty imitating George. She had him off to perfection. "And *junk mail*," Betty would add, "is two words, not one."

"Stop it," Pamela had pleaded, holding her ribs. Pamela had felt guilty, standing beside George's grave, chortling in such an abandoned way. "Poor old George," she had said, trying to put herself into a more respectful mood. To make obeisance, she had given his headstone a thorough polish.

Here lies George Arthur Higginbottom
1918–1997

"Passing through nature into the eternal"

Betty had said nothing, pursing her lips sceptically. Afterwards, the two of them had gone back to Betty's for tea.

Pamela came back to the present with a jolt as George's carriage clock suddenly struck six. She leapt from the settee as though stung for, since his demise, she had not wound the thing. It had been one of George's rituals and, somehow, it had seemed respectful, after his death, to let it rest too. She gingerly picked up the timepiece and held it to her ear. It was definitely ticking. How peculiar. Could it have been Betty, perhaps?

Bewildered, Pamela replaced the clock. It had been presented to George on his retirement from Braithwaite's Insurance, where he had worked for 43 years. Pamela yawned and considered returning to bed.

She was halfway to the stairs when the phone in the hall rang. She was close enough to silence it almost immediately, lifting the receiver to her ear. Nothing. After a while she could bear the eerie silence no longer.

"Who's there?" she demanded. "Will you stop ringing me!" With uncharacteristic force, she banged down the receiver.

This was something else that had begun following George's death. At first, she'd suspected someone who'd had a grudge against him – and there were certainly quite a number in that category. She and George had experienced nuisance calls in the past.

But this was different. She'd contacted BT, who had started monitoring her phone, although they insisted that there were no traces of calls at the times Pamela specified. Engineers had come and inspected the equipment, even replacing the handset itself, but the calls persisted, and often at very unsocial hours. *6.03am*, she wrote on the pad next to the handset.

That put paid to any more thought of sleep. She went to the kitchen and made herself another cuppa. It was still too early for breakfast and, anyway, the sandwich had satisfied her appetite.

"Oh, George," she sighed, putting down the spoon on the draining board. Though she thought she had done this carefully, the spoon somehow skittered off the edge of the sink and clattered into the metal recess.

"Clumsy!" Pamela admonished herself.

Back in the lounge, she crept past George's chair, observing his leather writing case lying neatly zipped on its shelf below the bookcase. His prized possession, a blue Parker 51 fountain pen, lay diagonally across the top. It was positioned not quite as he'd left it, for he'd had that fatal stroke and the pen, together with his writing pad and the board itself, had ended up on the floor alongside him.

As she walked by, Pamela once again tutted at the stubborn ink-stain on the carpet. It seemed to taunt her. She'd repeatedly tried to remove it but, although her efforts always seemed successful at first, the blue-black stain always reappeared. She was becoming resigned to it.

Betty maintained that it was how George would have wanted to go, still engaged in his one-man battle against the barbarians who were destroying the English language. These last words were decidedly George's, not Betty's. Pamela again smiled to herself, appreciative of Betty's skills at mimicry.

It was true, George often acted like an embattled warrior. When the post was due, for example, he would position himself at the bottom of the stairs, ready to pounce. George was always at his most tetchy when going through the mail. From the kitchen, she would hear him tutting or, occasionally, snorting with laughter. Though she tried to avoid being in the vicinity, George liked her to be present when he read his correspondence: to be his sounding board. All that was required of her were sympathetic noises – sighing, tutting, gasping – following his cue.

She now found herself ritualistically making these noises and laughed again. Betty was right. She needed to move on. Pamela sipped her tea thoughtfully, watching the light start to bleach the curtains.

She still received the occasional letter addressed to George, and it made her realise that, out there, others were continuing their rear-guard action against the new Dark Ages. She would always write back, letting the writer know that their fellow crusader had passed on. Except that she couldn't use that phrase: "passed on." George hated euphemisms. He always insisted on calling a spade "an implement for digging," which was another of his little jokes, of course. It was no surprise that many people didn't know what he was on about half the time.

He, though, had never been one to express any allegiance with fellow activists. George preferred to see himself as a lone wolf confronting an ignorant world, whether in the person of a local councillor, a journalist, or even unwitting innocents like Betty, with her incorrectly worded sign. Each could expect a strongly worded wrap on the knuckles. Some would write back, of course, defending themselves; or, more commonly, advising George what he might do with his pen, even one as valuable as a Parker 51.

Betty had suggested that Pamela might bury the pen with George, clipping it to the breast pocket of his best suit.

"It's not quite putting it where some of his respondents recommended," she'd said, "but he'd have his precious weapon with him in the hereafter, should he wish to get in contact."

She was a one!

Pamela leaned across George's chair and carefully unscrewed the top of his Parker. For some reason she'd started to check that it still contained ink; although, in his lifetime, George would never let her near it. She wasn't quite sure why she did this, especially given the stain on the carpet, but she proceeded to unzip his writing case and started doodling on the top sheet of his Basildon Bond pad. What would George say if he could see her, she wondered.

He used to tell her off for doodling in the margins of the newspaper. That was in the days when she tried to share his passion for the English language. She'd read out clues from the crossword to him, but she discovered that he wasn't actually very good at guessing the answers, preferring, instead, to criticise the compilers for their badly phrased clues. Despite the fact that she said doodling helped her think, George had always frowned on the practice.

As she recalled those early days of their marriage, she let George's pen flow across the pad more freely. She wrote his name several times, adding loops and flourishes.

She then discovered that, without even realising it, she had written the word "eternity" below his name. It was as though the pen, of its own volition, had come up with this word. She could have sworn, too, that the style of writing – especially those strong downstrokes – was more like George's hand.

Pamela almost dropped his pen in shock. She managed to hold on to it but, as her hand jerked, she blotted the paper, and the word "eternity" was partially lost beneath a bead of ink. She used the sheet of blotting paper at the front of the pad to absorb the spillage, but the last three letters were now unreadable.

"The moving finger writes, and having writ, moves on," he liked to quote at her. "And all your piety and wit cannot lure it back to cancel half a line, or all your tears wash out a word of it." She smiled to herself.

Her memory was still sound, at least. "The Rubaiyat of Omar Khayyam," she said aloud. She had always liked the sound of that.

Pamela went back to the kitchen to wash her stained fingers. But before she got there, the phone started jangling again. She lifted and dropped the handset in one movement, writing *6.22am* on the pad. Then, through the door, she watched as the bulb in the standard lamp, which stood behind George's chair, flicker several times before expiring with a little popping noise.

It was going to be one of those days. She went upstairs to run a bath. A long soak would do her good. She and Betty were going to visit the cemetery later, for it was exactly three months since George had died: three months since she had found him on the floor, his writing materials scattered about him.

☾❋☽

Later in the day, Pamela found herself clearing his plot of leaves and chocolate wrappers (George couldn't abide litter). She and Betty then sat side by side on a nearby bench, sharing a flask of tea and an iced bun.

"It's funny," said Betty, dispatching her last sticky mouthful, "that he wanted those words on his tombstone."

"What do you mean?" asked Pamela. "It's from one of his favourite plays. *Hamlet.*"

"That might be so, Pamela, but didn't he always hate ufo-whatsisnames?"

"Euphemisms?"

"That's them. Didn't he always hate it when people said 'passing' rather than 'dying'? Then he goes and has it on his tombstone."

"Headstone," Pamela couldn't stop herself correcting her friend. "Sorry," she smiled across at Betty. "A George moment." Pamela then seemed to register what her friend had said. "But you're right, Betty … how strange!" Why had she never noticed before?

Pamela took a mouthful of tea to clear her throat. "All I know is, when we were once at a performance of *Hamlet*, he turned to me and said that he thought it would make a most apposite epitaph." Pamela carefully screwed the top onto her thermos. "Passing through nature to eternity," she quoted.

"To the eternal," corrected Betty, pointing to the headstone.

"Oh, yes!" agreed Pamela, looking up. "Good job George isn't here!"

"I'm sure that if you'd buried him with his pen, you'd have received a letter post haste!"

They laughed.

That evening, after another cuppa at Betty's, Pamela went home. She was shocked to see the writing case lying unzipped and open on George's chair, with the pen alongside it, its top missing. Her heart thumped until she recalled the morning's upset. It must have been her.

Once again she caught sight of the word she'd unwittingly scrawled on his writing pad: *eternity*, now partially obliterated, and she recalled the Rubaiyat quote, too, about the impossibility of cancelling a word once writ. She chuckled to herself. What would George have said if he could have heard her? She screwed on the pen top and zipped up the writing case, placing the pen in its time-honoured position on top.

As she carefully arranged the items, she also noticed that the spines of George's reference books were out of line, particularly his precious *Oxford Book of Quotations*. Again, she was slightly startled, for she recalled straightening them earlier – another habit she'd picked up from him.

She reached out to realign this book – which George always referred to as his Bible – but, on a whim, removed it to check the *Hamlet* quotation. She knew it was there, for she remembered consulting it for the funeral director.

And there it was. Except that, it did indeed say "eternity", as she had correctly quoted it that afternoon. Which meant that – she swallowed hard – it was his headstone that was wrong.

☾✵☽

A fortnight later, Pamela and Betty were once again sitting together, drinking tea and eating ginger cake. This time they were at Pamela's, having just returned from their weekly trip to the cemetery. Pamela, in particular, was looking more relaxed, as Betty repeatedly told her.

The headstone had been changed, at Pamela's insistence, and it had cost her nothing, as the error turned out to lie with the stonemason. Pamela was convinced that this was the cause of all the disturbances she'd experienced. It was poor George, who just couldn't rest till things were put right.

Betty had simply laughed. But even she had to admit that things were now quieter in her neighbour's house and, what was more important, Pamela was now more at peace with herself.

As the two of them reflected on this, the phone suddenly rang. They clung to each other in shock. They looked ominously at the instrument before Betty shouted, looking heavenwards, "There's no need to thank her, George!"

Their laughter broke out again, drowning out the ringtone which, just as suddenly, halted.

A Vampire in Whitby

People have such a narrow stereotype when it comes to vampires. All they see are fanged incisors, drooling over a victim's jugular. Wandering through Whitby on the Halloween Goth Weekend, I could see hundreds of be-fanged youngsters disporting this look. I'd intended only a brief visit to the town, to see what all the fuss was about. But I was already weary of the spectacle and had decided, after a quick lunchtime drink, to move on.

I went into a pub called The Elsinore, thinking to escape, only to discover that the place was a key venue. It was as though I'd wandered onto the set of an expressionist film. The clientele was predominantly monochrome.

After I'd ordered a glass of Barolo, one of my favourite reds (I was impressed that they stocked it), the barman started to explain that the pub was named after Hamlet's castle, and that Bram Stoker had borrowed the name for his vampire hunter, Van Helsing.

"Why, though, does the pub sign feature a ship rather than a castle?" I asked the barman. He shrugged and turned to the next customer.

Of course, I'd visited Helsingør, the Danish island, several times, the first being on board a galleon somewhat similar to that pictured on their sign. That was long before the age of steam.

I went and found a seat. I have to admit, it was thanks to these Goths that I could sit in plain sight. With such walking clichés, no one would ever consider me a threat. The credit for this stereotype must go to the writer mentioned by the barman: Bram Stoker, a distant relative of mine. He was not the first to depict my kind, admittedly. Polidori, Le Fanu and *Varney the Vampire*'s authors had all done their bit, but it was Stoker who really put people off the scent: the idea that we can't bear sunlight – genius! That we have no reflection or shadow – brilliant! Let alone having those ridiculous fangs, or our supposed ability to transform into bats. Then there's the garlic, the fear of crucifixes and the rest.

Of course, the film industry leapt on the bandwagon, turning us into tall, debonair gents – think Bella Lugosi and Christopher Lee – complete with sexy Transylvanian accents, an immaculate dress code and slicked-back hair with that widow's peak. It was the perfect subterfuge.

So, I am eternally grateful to my Irish ancestor for his imaginative deception. It was the best sort of camouflage possible, even if more sympathetic portrayals have occasionally put it in jeopardy (I'm thinking of Anne Rice's *Interview with a Vampire* and that *Twilight* series). But they're still a minority. Looking around at the young Goths in The Elsinore, with their piercings, pasty faces and kohl eyes, the stereotype was secure.

The Barolo was delicious. We vampires have to be very careful about how much alcohol we imbibe (a fact we do not advertise), but I could not resist a second glass. Barolo is made from the Nebbiolo, a small, thick-skinned and fleshy grape. It looks disappointing, but when you bite into it, its juice, rich in tannins, squirts out like … well, like you know what. Barolo's garnet colour always brings this image to mind.

It was quite a crush returning to my seat. "Watch out, mister," a young male hailed me, "or you'll drop your Vimto!"

"Barolo," I replied, not familiar with the wine he mentioned, "from the Piedmont region of Italy."

"Vimto," the chap replied, "from t' Pennine region o' Lancashire." His friends guffawed.

For an instant, my eyes flared, but I managed to restrain myself, forcing a smile as I eased myself back into my seat.

He hardly gave me a second look (this is how well I pass unnoticed) so I was able to study him and his companions more closely. Underneath all that make-up, the piercings, tattoos and flamboyant hair, Vimto man was an attractive specimen: firm-fleshed and long-limbed. Next to him sat an equally attractive female, breasts pushed high, eyes bright green in kohl surrounds. I would, I confess, willingly invite both to support my favourite cause: to become blood donors, giving blood generously (it's an old joke, I know).

Although I thought I was being circumspect, I must have been staring, for Vimto man addressed me again: "You want a closer look, Mr Barolo?"

I was embarrassed. I shook my head, my hands making apologetic gestures. People today are so forward, the young especially.

Others at the table had now taken up his suggestion that I join them. It was becoming awkward, so I decided to comply. And, I must admit, these youngsters intrigued me. In fact, to be brutally honest, I had been feeling lonely of late.

"You are most generous," I said, shifting my chair.

"I wouldn't say that," replied Vimto man. "It's your round."

They laughed, but I didn't mind. I was happy to indulge them.

"If one of you will do the honours, I'll willingly purchase more drinks." I extracted a couple of twenties from my wallet and passed them over.

Of course, another glass of Barolo arrived for me. Vimto man had remembered my tipple. I was impressed. But I really had to be careful with my consumption. Our blood chemistry is particularly complex and sensitive.

The company was convivial, I'll say that. Behind the monochrome façade, they were a lively bunch. I've always had a soft spot for the young, their energy and passion, let alone their firm young flesh.

Though the conversation was generally light and frivolous, they did ask me some personal questions. I spun them one of my standard biographies – one generally popular with the young – about my involvement in the film business, working for Hammer Horror. It was a background that somehow justified my fascination with their look.

After another drink ("No more for me," I'd insisted), I was invited back to where they were staying. As I learnt on the way, Belle Addison, the young lady with green eyes, lived with her Uncle Murdo, who, on Goth Weekends, held open house.

His house turned out to be more of a mansion, one of the few Victorian properties still standing in an isolated crescent of modern houses. For a band of Goths, it was an apposite niche, more atmospheric than many of the official festival venues.

As I crossed the threshold, I gave a chuckle, to acknowledge that I'd been officially invited in. (I should perhaps add that, contrary to the stereotype, this is another myth. We vampires can go where we like, invited or not; but, being a refined, courteous race, we wouldn't dream of intruding where we were not welcome.)

As her friends dispersed to the various rooms, Belle gave me a personal tour. Inside, the place was quite modern but, with various drapes and candles, she and her friends had created a Gothic feel more in keeping with the property's exterior. Old paintings and curios added to the atmosphere. It was perfect for Halloween. In fact, it would have been perfect for a Hammer film, too.

Though I felt somewhat out of place, the partygoers seemed to accept me as a harmless eccentric. Of course, they knew little of my ulterior motives. (I had already identified one or two potential donors.)

In the library, I was introduced to Uncle Murdo, sitting at an ornate desk and reading a newspaper. We exchanged pleasantries but that was all. He didn't question my presence. From the library we returned to the kitchen, where others were enjoying some soup and crusty bread that a housekeeper was distributing. I took a bowl myself.

People then gravitated to the lounge where some loud music was playing. It was not really my "thing", especially given my sensitive ears, but I put up with it, surreptitiously inserting some protectors, and continued to observe them all talking, smoking, reading, even dancing. I learnt they were saving their energies for a night on the town, though a few had retired, the worse for wear after lunchtime at The Elsinore.

It's difficult to know what attracts one to a particular individual, but Belle fascinated me. With that raven-black hair and those piercing green eyes – courtesy of tinted contact lenses, I realised – she was undoubtedly attractive. Beyond that, there was a vulnerability about her, which I'll always associate with her scent. A vampire's sense of smell is as acute as his hearing and, if I was not mistaken, Belle was AB negative, that rarest of blood groups, possessed by just one percent of humans.

I could sense those corpuscles calling to me. So, when she went upstairs, I followed her, maintaining a discreet distance. It wasn't just for selfish reasons, either. I was concerned at the way she was swaying.

When she turned into a bedroom, I remained on the landing, admiring the collection of prints that adorned Murdo's walls. After a few minutes, I heard a small gasp. I moved to her doorway. Through her mirror, I could see her sitting at a dressing table, a short, ivory-handled blade in her right hand, tracing arabesques on her left arm. I could almost feel the systole-diastole shunt as a rivulet of blood snaked to her wrist.

I ran in and grabbed her arm, staunching the flow above her elbow. I could now see that, from elbow to wrist, her flesh was ridged with scar tissue. I knelt and applied my tongue to this latest cut, fastening my lips round it. Like nectar, the rare substance slipped down my throat.

All too soon, the coagulant in my saliva inhibited the flow. My joke about being a blood donor was not fanciful. We are biologically limited to something close to the NHS quota. None of that ridiculous nonsense about sucking our hosts dry. As if any parasite would destroy its provider.

Moreover, I hope none of you are taken in by that drivel about vampires creating more of their kind by biting humans. I mean, would you expect a human to turn into a horse after being bitten by one? As some mathematician once worked out, if it took a mere bite, vampires would dominate the world by now.

Even though it's ludicrous to think of our bites as reproductive devices, they do have one other feature of note. Namely, our salivary glands contain an anaesthetic, such that our hosts recall nothing of their donation; apart, that is, from what I've been reliably informed is an extremely pleasurable high.

However, with Belle, something clearly went awry, for while *she* emitted a contented moan, *I* felt most peculiar: disoriented and woozy. The alcohol might have been a factor, but I was convinced there was more to it. Were there, I wondered, other substances in her system: marijuana, cocaine … ecstasy?

That was my last conscious thought before I crashed onto her bed. How could she have polluted such a fine vintage? It was like adding fizzy pop to a classic malt!

❦

When I woke, I was shocked to discover that I was not alone. A group of Goths had gathered round me, Belle amongst them, her arms now shielded from view. All were looking down at me, beaming inanely. Vimto man then produced a mirror, which he angled towards my face. Were they testing me, I wondered, to see if I cast a reflection? What had Belle told them?

I glanced in the mirror, vaguely anxious lest my image not be there (it's so easy to be seduced by the media stereotype). With hindsight, I think I'd have been less surprised by its absence than by what confronted me. My face was a nightmare. Caked in make-up, it resembled a clown's. It was predominantly white with stark black eyes, above which false eyebrows, rising like miniature Gothic arches, had been etched. And above them, my hairline now featured a widow's peak. As for my lips, they were purple, with a pair of those iconic fangs protruding. Traces of blood marbled them, with a trail of red trickling down to my neck. Had Belle said something? I glanced at her, but she gave nothing away. Like the rest, she just smiled.

The indignity! Did they not know with whom they were dealing? Were they not aware that I could strike them down in an instant? I was about to cast the mirror aside and berate them when I spotted something else. I reached up a hand to confirm it. Yes. On my right eardrum there was a silver stud. Not that the type of metal was a problem (another myth, of course), but the idea that they'd taken such liberties with my person while I was unconscious was highly disturbing. I felt molested, defiled! For the first time in my long life, I was the one who'd been, well … penetrated!

"What do you think of our makeover?" enquired Vimto man.

"You've certainly been busy," was all I could manage. "How long have I been … out?"

"Hours," they said.

"Now you won't feel such an outsider," said someone else.

I could do nothing but smile at the irony, innocents that they were. The spectacle over, they wandered off, chuckling to each other; even Belle seemed coy.

My first thought was that I should leave immediately. After all, I'd intended only a brief visit to the town. However, when I went downstairs, my "fellow" Goths were so keen to have me with them that I felt I could not let them down, especially given the trouble they'd taken in preparing me.

They were the first humans, I realised, with whom I'd had any interaction in decades (apart from the obvious). The prospect of resuming my ceaseless globetrotting suddenly held no attraction. I therefore agreed to accompany them, especially as I had this Goth mask to hide behind.

❨✹❩

The evening was not particularly eventful – pubs, festival venues, some promenading around the sites – but their companionship was a boon. They reminded me of the young Romantics I'd encountered back in the 1790s. They too had rejected the conventions of the day, seeking isolated spots like the Abbey ruins. And they, also, were forever exploring altered states of consciousness, using alcohol and other recreational substances.

But what really brought the Romantics to mind was the way these Goths rejected violence, albeit it seemed to breed aggression in others. For this reason, I was pleased to be able to offer them some protection. Another irony!

There were a few occasions when I'd had to take aside some rowdy locals, politely advising them to stand down. Despite their initial oaths and braggadocio, they soon found my grip and penetrating stare persuasive; perhaps my facial makeover also helped. "Barolo the Minder," my new friends started calling me.

That evening certainly did me a lot of good, making me realise what a hermit I'd become. It was unnerving to be so visible amongst such crowds, but it was therapeutic. Strangers even stopped me for selfies. Invisible behind my mask, I was happy to comply.

❦

It is now over a year since that madcap weekend and I find myself in Whitby still, the guest of Belle and her uncle. We make an odd threesome, but then this town is a place where eccentrics of all stripes have found sanctuary.

After that first memorable night, I had intended to move on, but my heart wasn't in it, particularly as Belle and her Goth friends had made me so welcome. Despite our age differences (to put it mildly), they were very tolerant and, I must say, I have come to develop a sympathy for their attitude to life. I've even started to adopt their style of dress and appearance – and the silver stud is still in place.

Murdo and I have also found we have much in common. Ever since I'd heard about him holding an open house for the young, I'd had my suspicions. Not that we ever talk openly about such things. It's an unspoken code amongst our kind.

Belle, it turns out, was the first runaway for whom Murdo had provided sanctuary (they are not related at all, of course). I'm pleased to say that she is now far more stable, studying for a university place. She certainly has no new scars – a few puncture marks, admittedly, but these, I assure you, are therapeutic only. You must think of my treatment regime in medical terms, like administering methadone shots to a drug addict – except that my treatment provides a more rewarding high.

Please don't get the wrong idea. My own habit, as we might call it, is gratified elsewhere. I now have a job. It arose out of that memorable Goth night. Some of the officials asked whether I might help with security on a regular basis. I was delighted to offer my services. Anything to support the local community – and I have been doing so ever since.

So do, please, come along. You'll be made most welcome, I can assure you. It'll be an experience you'll never forget!

The Girl in Room 39

A young woman with shoulder-length auburn hair walks across his room. Apart from a silver chain on her left wrist, she is naked, her back to him. A delicate fragrance fills the air. She glides over to the en suite, pushing open the door and swinging it shut behind her. He finds her unexpectedly arousing.

Then he wakes. It is the fifth night in a row he's dreamt of her and, strangest of all, the dream replicates his waking reality. There he is, lying in bed, looking at the bathroom door that she went through. It's shut, although he's convinced that, as on former nights, he'd left it open.

As on those previous occasions, Graeme feels compelled to get up and search his en suite, to make sure that, after all, it was only a dream; that there is no woman, naked or otherwise, lurking in his bathroom. Not, as he tells himself, that he would particularly welcome one.

It is this aspect that most disturbs Graeme: the way her presence excites him. After years of uncertainty, he thought he'd finally come to terms with his sexuality. He's never officially "come out", as people term it, never having felt any need to do so. And perhaps he was wise not to, he now thinks, given how alluring he finds this figure conjured from his subconscious.

Graeme can't get back to sleep. In the end, he gives up, showers and dresses in his white shirt, blue tie and grey suit. After checking himself in the mirror – blond curly hair, blue eyes, cheeky grin – he makes his way downstairs, stopping *en route* to greet the housekeeping staff, who, as usual, are gathered around the linen closet.

On the ground floor, he pops in to see the kitchen staff too, before taking a seat in the restaurant. This is his favourite time of day, watching the early diners impetuously consume breakfasts before shooting off to work. With Christmas imminent, there are fewer such guests. Still, Graeme pays attention to their eating habits, their use of the self-service stations, their interactions with hotel staff.

After his own, more leisurely breakfast, Graeme checks his watch. Mandy, Mr Venables' secretary, should be arriving shortly. He goes through to her office and sits himself at her desk, such that, when she enters, he appears to be tapping away at her keyboard, sporting her computer glasses. Exactly as he's observed her do, he raises his eyes to Mandy, pushing the specs up the bridge of his nose.

"Graeme!" she exclaims, giggling at his cheeky impression. "I almost dropped my cappuccino."

"Sorry, Mands."

"If Mr Venables catches you, you'll be for it!"

Almost involuntarily, Graeme glances up at the framed picture of Mr Reginald Venables on the wall. The hotel's owner, corpulent and stocky, stands imperiously in the portico of The Excelsior. He looks so proud of his independent establishment, founded by his grandfather, who can be seen in an adjacent black-and-white photo, similarly posed. In turn, this bearded patriarch is framed alongside Reginald's father. Only the vagaries of fashion distinguish the three generations of Venables.

"Don't look so worried!" says Mandy. "You know he can't afford to lose you. You've turned this place around and he knows it." Graeme's smile returns. "Why else do you think he gave you a room here?"

"So I can work even longer hours?" answers Graeme. Mandy laughs appreciatively, until Graeme adds, "And it *is* room 39!"

They exchange knowing glances. Room 39 was the only one not to be redecorated, having become something of a lumber room. When it was offered to Graeme, other staff made sure he heard the rumours: about it being haunted; about someone being attacked in there; about a drowning in the bath; about a suicide.

Graeme, forever a Pollyanna, had brushed off such gossip. He'd leapt at the chance to establish himself away from his tyrannical father. He'd had the room cleared and quickly personalised it. The only mistake he'd made was trying to enlist Arthur's help, not realising at the time that Arthur did nothing without Mr Venables' explicit say-so – and even then, reluctantly.

Graeme and Mandy have a quick look over the Christmas programme before Graeme takes his leave, walking out into the freshly decorated foyer where he admires the festive tree, his own handiwork. He's purchased a proper one and freshened up the decorations and lights, adding a stack of brightly wrapped boxes beneath. Safely stored elsewhere, there are presents for each guest and member of staff.

Graeme had a huge battle with Mr Venables over this extravagance, but, as the Facebook pictures and comments show, Graeme's presence has garnered nothing but positive reviews – as Mandy is only too aware. Amongst young and old alike, Graeme is Mr Popular. He knows all the established residents by name and indulges their every whim and foible. As for the kids, they adore him and his funny walks and face pulling, his willingness to participate in their games.

Generally, Graeme's a happy man. He loves his job, he relishes his new independence and, most importantly, he feels at peace with himself – albeit these recent dreams have upset his equilibrium.

They are not nightmares, of course. In fact, many people would be envious of having a beautiful naked woman waltzing through their room night after night; that chestnut hair, the trim buttocks and long, lithe legs. But, for Graeme himself, the fact that she turns him on is precisely the problem.

Though Graeme finds his dreams troubling, he is even more upset when, two days later, they cease. He still wakes at 4.15 a.m.; still looks around for her. Has he, perhaps, slept through her appearance, he wonders, before catching up with himself, realising he's confusing dream and reality. Even so, he feels a need to check the bathroom, just in case.

Two nights after the naked girl's final visitation, Graeme has another dream, also set in his room. It's almost a sequel. In this one, he finds himself lying in bed listening to the sound of taps running. When he wakes, it takes him several minutes to realise that the sound persists. He goes through to the en suite, to discover both bath taps going full tilt. The room is steaming up. Once again, it is 4.15 a.m.

Graeme silences the taps and pulls the lever to release the plug. It doesn't respond. It is jammed in some way. Graeme crawls back to bed. He'll attend to it in the morning.

This second dream recurs the following night and, once again, Graeme wakes to the sound of the bath filling. He can't understand it. He'd checked the taps scrupulously before going to bed. Once again, it's 4.15 a.m. This time he rises more swiftly, to prevent an overflow. As on the previous night, by morning the water has drained away.

Because of the elusive nature of the problem, Graeme has been reluctant to involve others. But after his third rude awakening he's desperate. Lying wide-eyed in bed, he takes more seriously the rumours he's heard, especially the one about the suicide in the bath. Could the tub possess some sort of malevolent consciousness, like a Stephen King monster? Could the naked girl be its handmaiden, a mermaid of some kind who entices people into the water and drags them under?

As it gets lighter, Graeme manages to look at things more rationally, returning to the notion that the girl is a projection of his subconscious – a manifestation, perhaps, of his sexual confusion. Even so, the water is inescapably real, for which he needs a plumber. Then, maybe, he can attend to his more personal concerns.

After breakfast, he seeks out Arthur. Graeme's never been down to the handyman's subterranean realm before, and Arthur certainly doesn't encourage visitors. Why, wonders Graeme, does Venables keep him on? The man is a law unto himself.

It takes Graeme several minutes to track down Arthur. He finally locates him sitting by the boiler with his feet on a table, drinking from a mug of tea and reading the *Daily Mail*.

Arthur is not pleased to be discovered, and even less so to have his "break" interrupted. He merely grunts from behind his paper when Graeme asks him to look at a faulty bath outlet. When Graeme adds that it's room 39, though, Arthur's manner changes. His fingers start to tremble, his paper rustles. After a lengthy pause, Arthur demurs, declaring that it's a job for a professional.

Graeme, though, has anticipated this response. He drops a maintenance form (one of his many innovations) behind Arthur's newspaper defences. "Mr Venables specially requests it," Graeme announces. He has had the foresight to get his boss to sign a batch of these forms up-front.

Back upstairs, Graeme wanders out to the portico, mesmerised by heavy flakes of falling snow. After the fug of Arthur's subterranean lair, it is refreshingly cool. The snow is coming down steadily. It has already begun to gift wrap the cars and street furniture. Graeme smiles. Such a fall can only enhance business, he knows. Guests will stay in, drinking and eating their way through the Christmas break.

As he makes his way back, Graeme suddenly senses someone beside him, though he'd spotted no one approaching. A tallish young woman is there. She's wearing a short, dark-blue jacket and black bucket hat, beneath which her brown hair is tucked.

"This is the Excelsior, isn't it?" she asks. Graeme nods. "I wondered if there was any Christmas work?"

She has a strong face with striking cheekbones. Her voice is unexpectedly rich and resonant. Graeme is startled at how attractive he finds her. What is happening to him?

Normally, he would refer potential staff to Mandy, but something about this woman makes him hesitate. He wants to prolong their interaction, to understand the way he feels.

He leads her into the restaurant, now quiet after the breakfast rush. They go through the usual questions, about her experience of hotel work, her schooling and qualifications. Later, though, all Graeme can recall is her name: "Krissy, with a K."

What is it about her that is so alluring? He tries to parse his feelings but, once again, fails. Clichés prevail. He just wants to keep her talking so that he can continue to gaze at her, bathe in that delightful smile, wallow in the bottomless pools of her eyes.

To prolong their interaction, Graeme suggests a tour. He proposes they start on the top floor and work down. But he steers her past the lifts. For some reason he wants to avoid Mandy and other members of staff. He wants to keep Krissy to himself.

On the back stairs, he finds himself hanging back, enjoying her ascent, the graceful sway of her figure.

But he is also disturbed by something. Is it that blue jacket? It suits her, but it's too light for this weather – unless she's come by car. Her cotton trousers as well, too thin, although he is enjoying the motion of her glutes, rhythmically flexing.

It's not long before they are strolling along the top corridor, passing his room. Should he let her see it? He's aware that room 39 is not typical, but he can't show her any of the other rooms because he hasn't checked Reception to see if any are vacant. Besides, he hasn't his passkey with him. Krissy, though, picks up on his hesitancy. She gestures towards the door, asking if they might see inside.

"Of course," Graeme says.

The room, he is relieved to see, is not too untidy. However, once they are inside, he is surprised to detect the lingering scent of his nocturnal visitor. He hadn't smelled that for a while.

He thinks she too must have noticed when she remarks, "Someone's already in this one." But it's his collection of shirts that she's indicating, suspended on hangers around the picture rail.

"No worries," he chuckles. "Those are, er … mine."

As their increasingly intimate chat proceeds, Graeme becomes aware of the sound of water. He groans and moves towards the en suite, swinging open the door. They both stare at the liquid cascading over the side of the tub. Once again Graeme rattles the plug mechanism. It won't budge. He tries to turn off the taps, the spouts of which are already submerged. But the taps are in the off position.

Where *is* the water coming from?

He throws some towels on the floor and looks round for a receptacle of some sort, then remembers the flower vase on his desk. He turns to ask Krissy to fetch it, but she's disappeared. Perhaps gone for help, he surmises. He fetches the vase and energetically ladles water from the bath into the toilet, feeling like the Sorcerer's Apprentice.

No one appears. Graeme runs to the bedside phone and rings Arthur direct. No civilities this time. He orders him to come up immediately, giving the emergency code, though he does emphasise that it's on Mr Venables' say so.

Armed with a bag of tools, Arthur appears with surprising alacrity. He looks different: old and vulnerable.

Graeme asks, "Did you see …?"

"You've 'ad a visitor, 'aven't you?" Arthur interrupts. His tone is part accusatory, part remorseful. "I know that smell." He says no more and makes his way through to the en suite.

Graeme leaves him to it. He phones Mandy and explains what's happened, suggesting that the rooms beneath 39 be checked.

It is only a few minutes before Arthur staggers back from the bathroom, arms and face dripping. In his hand he holds a silver chain. "There," he says, dropping a slimy bracelet into Graeme's hand. "Jamming the mechanism."

Arthur's hands are shaking again, Graeme notices.

Sitting on his bed, Graeme looks up at Arthur, who suddenly seems a broken man. Graeme realises that the water running down his face is not from the bath. Once again, Graeme recalls the stories he's been told. With this chain in his hand – which he immediately recognises as similar to the one worn by his dream walker – he starts to take more seriously the notion that the room is haunted.

The thought does not scare him. He simply wants to understand. Somehow Arthur is involved. Had he attacked some young woman here? Had he drowned her in this very tub?

Graeme tries to articulate his thoughts: "So she –," he begins, but Arthur once again interrupts.

"HE!" he shouts. "*He*! My son!" He flops down on the bed beside Graeme, gesturing for Graeme to look at the chain.

Brushing the greenish patina from the identity plate, Graeme reads: "Christopher, Love Mum and Dad."

Arthur, eyes fixed on the floor, tells Graeme about Christopher, whom he, Arthur, had spurned when the boy told him that he should've been a girl; that he was going for gender reassignment. Arthur tells Graeme how depressed and confused his son had been, and how he, his one-and-only Dad, had refused to listen. How his son, desperate and lost and lonely, had booked in here, into this very room. How he had ended his life in this very bath. How his wife, Susan, had blamed him, and left him. How his other two children wouldn't speak to him.

"Six years ago this Christmas," Arthur concludes, his belligerent tone briefly reasserting itself. "And on this, of all days, you call me up here to fix the soddin' *bath*!" He falters in sobs and tears.

Graeme is stunned. He'd got it wrong. Christopher was … a *boy*! He can't suppress the smile that briefly lights up his face.

Graeme stands up and places a tentative hand on one of Arthur's heaving shoulders. "It'll get better … now that you're … letting it out."

Graeme realises he's wittering. He thrusts the chain back into Arthur's hand and says, "Krissy's." He immediately bites his tongue and amends the word to "Christopher's." Graeme's profound sense of relief is making it difficult to focus on Arthur's tragic loss.

"You mean well," begins Arthur, "for one of those …"

"Alright, Arthur!" interrupts another voice. Mr Venables and Mandy are standing in the doorway.

☾❀☽

The following morning Graeme wakes early from an undisturbed night's sleep. Venables had offered him another room – despite their being full to capacity –

but Graeme turned it down. He's content where he is, subject to a lick or two of paint, as he has pointed out.

This morning he feels in need of something more immersive than a shower, but he certainly doesn't want to use his own bath. He goes down to the pool instead – closed to guests at this time of day – and swims till his body feels loose and unknotted.

Back in his room, he pampers himself with some Dior *Sauvage* before picking out his powder-blue suit, which he wears over a buttermilk shirt, paisley tie and matching pocket square.

On his way downstairs, he catches sight of the housekeeping staff at the end of the corridor and quickly conceals himself in their linen closet. Donning the regulation mob cap and tabard, he awaits his moment before leaping out at them, striking a dramatic pose. They squeal and giggle, despite the unsocial hour.

At his insistence they join him outside the closet for a collective selfie. It's one he'll always treasure. And later in the day, he'll forward it to friends and family, adding a few carefully chosen words.

One day, he might even send a copy to his father.

Rest in Peace

George tried not to cry out when he heard the rap at his door. He was hiding under the bedclothes, a pillow wedged either side of his head. Even so, he could still hear the steady tramp of feet along the corridor. It was always worse in the afternoons, he'd noticed.

Why wouldn't they leave him alone, these ghosts from the trenches? Endlessly, they moved through the house, looking round like zombies, unaware that death had already claimed them, not realising they were trapped in Purgatory as a punishment for the part they'd played in that conflict. And they weren't just English victims, either. George had distinctly caught the sound of foreign tongues – German ones, even!

Early on, when George first became conscious of their presence, he'd found that they, by contrast, were unaware of him. He could walk straight through them. Like wraiths, they were, dispersing at his approach. After discovering some of them loitering in his personal water closet, he'd thought they were everywhere, but then he'd found his old bedroom was a refuge. Apart from the occasional rattle or rap – the sort of thing you might hear at those popular spiritualist gatherings – they let him be.

He still could not believe, though, that the rest of his family were deaf to this marauding army. Then again, weren't they also oblivious to the servants' presence? With embarrassment, George recalled how, as children, they'd bounced on this very bed while the poor maid struggled to change the sheets.

There'd been ten of them, and he'd been the youngest (Baby to his siblings). His childhood had been one long idyllic summer of boating, cricket and parties – endless parties. In those days the house was teeming with life. There was music and games, carriages queuing outside and servants forever bustling.

George recalled running up and down the long gallery, weaving through the guests as they stood around in their finery and, much to their amusement, his heroic big brother, Thomas, would chase him. In many ways, now he came to think of it, it was like that once again, having to thread your way through the zombie-like crowds loitering in the gallery, gawping at his family's possessions.

Poor Thomas, or Tommy as he was always known. Had he lived, he'd now be the seventh Viscount. Tragically, he'd bought it at the Battle of Loos in 1915, where George himself had been wounded. They all told George he was the lucky one, but it certainly didn't feel that way, living on in this mausoleum, with that endless stream of ghosts everywhere.

That wasn't quite fair. There were still two of his sisters and one brother, Arthur, who lived here and cared for him as best they could. They were very proud of their Baby, who had also been awarded the Military Cross for gallantry. George himself, though, thought the whole military exercise a futile disaster.

Life in the trenches had changed him profoundly. Leaving aside his own brother, there were thousands of other Tommies out there. Those undernourished men who'd served under him, wreathed in cigarette smoke, their smiles disquieting, each with a mouth full of decay and ruin, like no-man's-land.

Only Wilfred Owen's poetry, recently published, gave George any succour these days. It had inspired him to write about the war. The doctors had told him it was therapeutic. But the rhythms of his verse, he'd found, were continually disrupted by the hordes tramping through the family home – especially in the afternoons.

In the trenches, the afternoons had generally been a quiet time, before the dreaded "stand to" at dusk, when attacks were imminent. Nights were a frenzy of activity: digging trenches, repairing barbed wire, killing rats. Even now, George couldn't rest at nights. He felt a compulsion to wander the house, checking its defences, auditing supplies.

He knew the family thought him barmy – "shell shocked", as they termed it. It perplexed him that none of them could hear the relentless tread of these walking dead. Perhaps it was only after you yourself had been close to death that you became attuned to these souls in limbo. He was thankful, nevertheless, to be whole in body, unlike some of his friends, disfigured beyond recognition: Bertie Carter-Wallace with his prosthetic nose; Charles Carruthers with no legs.

George often felt ashamed of being so self-centred. "Pull yourself together," Arthur was always telling him. "Occupy yourself!"

But what hadn't he tried? Gardening, basket-weaving, painting, pottery, writing. How many nursing homes had he been in? Medication, recreational activities, rest cures – all such a waste of time.

Just then, there was another thump at the door. Like a starter's pistol, it galvanised George. He stood, resolute. During the war, he'd witnessed others react this way. In those days he'd been the spectator, watching aghast as a lone soldier would suddenly hurl himself over the top.

❀

Somewhat deferentially, the local newspaper reported that twenty-four-year-old George Moreton-Crumby, the war veteran, had accidentally fallen from a third-storey window at the family's home.

Some forty years later, the same paper would report that the family's magnificent estate had been gifted to the National Trust by its last surviving member, Arthur Reginald Moreton-Crumby. As part of their tour, visitors to the property would have the spot pointed out where George had plunged to his death in 1920. Those more psychically inclined would claim they could still detect the aura of an unhappy spirit.

As for George's bedroom, it was not open to visitors. Some, attracted precisely by the room's dark past, were disappointed. And the occasional tourist couldn't resist trying the door, rattling the handle, or rapping on the panelling, frustrated at the family's stipulation that this room should remain forever locked in order that their dear, mentally disturbed brother might, finally – they hoped – come to rest in peace.

The Fall and Rise of Albert Palmerson

This is the strange story of my uncle, the writer Albert Palmerson, who died peacefully over fifteen years ago. I should put peacefully in scare quotes because Uncle Albert maintained that he died for the first time twelve years prior to this, and far less calmly.

Bizarre, I know, but let me tell you his version of the story, which was brought freshly to mind after reading an article in this week's *Sunday Times* about a celebrated young poet. I should say that I never heard Uncle tell his own tale in one straight narrative. I'd catch bits and pieces, often after he'd had a drink or three. Some of what he said I've been able to corroborate elsewhere, but certainly not the crucial elements – and I doubt they ever could be.

Let me start with his background. Albert Palmerson was of medium height and build. He had a prominent chin and a high wide forehead. By the time I first became aware of him (in my teens), his hair was already a steely grey. Most distinctively, he was severely short-sighted, and most of the time wore a pair of old-fashioned pebble specs.

When asked, he would always describe himself a writer, but, from what publishers have told me, early on he was in danger of entering the *Guinness Book of Records* as one of the most rejected authors ever. The irony, which has been expressed by several publishers, is that his writing was not in itself bad. In fact, many maintain that, in technical terms, it was almost faultless (albeit of a rather prolix, Jamesian cast).

The problems lay elsewhere. Firstly, with the content of his prose, which was unrelentingly dark. God forbid that anyone with a depressed cast of mind should encounter it! But as none of this early work was ever published, this was not really a concern. As his relative, I was one of the few who ever read it, and I think I've survived unscathed.

Pessimism, though, wasn't the main problem. After all, other authors are renowned for their melancholy take on life: Hardy, Kafka and Beckett come to mind. But none of these had my uncle's volatile nature. At the slightest whiff of criticism, he was on the offensive.

So it was the publishers' anonymous readers and their editors who received his flack. Off would go the readers' reports to my uncle and, usually by return of post, back would come one of Uncle's infamous diatribes – pages of it, all in blotchy longhand – fulminating against their pedestrian attempts to stifle his creative voice. Editors, in particular, he regarded as nothing but jumped-up, failed authors who took their frustrations out on those more blessed with creative genes.

It's at this point that my uncle's story turns a bit spooky. But perhaps I should tell you one more thing before we go there. Namely, that Albert Palmerson was brought up Catholic and, at one time, had considered entering the church. However, this idea came to a sudden end when his very first piece of creative writing was rejected by the parish magazine, though the editor did provide copious suggestions as to how Albert's story might be improved.

Even though he was, at the time, a young, inexperienced writer, Uncle resented this attempt – as he saw it – to curb his independence of mind. He complained not just to the magazine editor, but to the parish priest and, subsequently, to the bishop of the diocese. The original letters have long been lost, but those involved have described his correspondence as not merely offensive but also blasphemous. Perhaps not surprisingly, Uncle forsook the church and, from then on, those pebble glasses of his beheld nothing that wasn't at least half-empty of meaning.

Chartered accountancy – or "rendering stuff to Caesar", as Uncle liked to describe it – was to become his day job, but he still devoted his evenings to writing those unpublishable novels and collecting rejection slips.

He wasn't a complete anorak, though. He also liked to tend his garden, which was the cause of his downfall and the weird event I keep putting off relating. So, let's get on with it.

According to my uncle, he was out in his garden, up his favourite apple tree pruning a few branches when he fell. It wasn't a particularly high tree, but he landed badly, crashing down onto his wheelbarrow. Even that wouldn't have been too bad had his scythe not been standing in the barrow at the time, its curved blade pointing skywards.

He landed on his back and the scythe sliced effortlessly through him. He recalled the blade emerging from his abdomen "like a shark's fin". I've seen the scars on his torso, back and front, so can vouch for this, but it's what happened afterwards that's the contentious part, the part that no one can corroborate. In what follows, then, I'm dependent on Uncle's account, related not just personally, but also in a fictionalised version that he was later to publish.

There was my uncle, skewered in his wheelbarrow with a shark fin sprouting from his abdomen. He always maintained that, at this point, he died. He didn't simply "lose consciousness" or "go into a coma" but actually *died*. He was adamant about this.

The next thing he knew, he was climbing a carved stairway towards the Pearly Gates. Alongside them, next to one of the bejewelled pillars that supported the gates, stood a man in a long white robe.

"St Peter, I presume," my uncle said, spotting the keys.

"Yes, my son," replied St Peter. "We had high hopes for you at one time, and would have welcomed your arrival. Sadly, that's changed. You are now destined for elsewhere."

"Why? What did I do?" demanded my uncle.

"It's more what you *didn't* do," responded St Peter. "Life is about growth and development. You, though, have systematically spurned the advice of others, never learning anything. Do you disagree? Have you ever heeded anyone's counsel?"

"I would gladly have done so had I been advised of anything that wasn't half-baked nonsense!"

"'The way of a fool is right in his own eyes. But he that harkeneth unto counsel, is wise.' Perhaps you know the quotation? Proverbs, 12:15. A little humility would not go amiss, my son."

"So this, I presume, is yet another rejection I'm hearing?" said Uncle, once again taking the initiative.

At this point St Peter and his Pearly Gates faded away. Before my uncle could decide what was happening, the air cleared and another pair of gates materialised. They were not pearly at all but gunmetal grey with bent, rusty spikes on top. The gates also leaned into each other, gaping wide at the bottom as though long neglected. Unlike the former gates, this kingdom clearly had no named keeper of the keys. Instead, Uncle found himself staring at a small, red-hued figure with budding horns on his forehead and, in one hand, a trident, the prongs of which were also bent and rusty.

Again, Uncle took the initiative. "I always thought the entrance to Hades was a gaping maw – a 'hellmouth' in fact."

"We've come a long way since the Middle Ages," replied the demon.

Uncle Albert decided not to argue. In his writings, he'd often tried to depict hell, so was keen to see how it looked in reality. He began walking towards the yawning gates.

"And where do you think you're going?"

"Baaa!" responded my Uncle, right into the demon's face. "Having failed as a sheep, I thought I'd explore my goatishness."

"Very witty, Mr Palmerson. But we don't automatically accept rejects from … up there," replied the demon, his eyes flickering upwards.

"Oh. I thought you had a niche for everyone here."
Uncle gave his impression of a lift operative: "Going
up, first floor – fornicators, pagans, suicides …"

"This isn't the *Divine Comedy*! If we took in all that
shower, we'd need far bigger premises!"

"So, who does get to stay in your exclusive, long-stay
accommodation?"

"You have to have been *really* wicked. A murderer,
rapist, war criminal or the like. An impenitent baddy."

"And arsonists? I bet you've a soft spot for them,"
joked Uncle, but the demon was unamused. "So,"
Uncle continued, "is this yet another cold shoulder I'm
being given? Another rejection?" Still the demon said
nothing. "What would you have me do?" demanded
Uncle, exasperated.

The demon finally responded, "After consultation
with the boys upstairs," again he flicked up his eyes,
"we've decided that you're another of these lukewarm
idlers who grumble endlessly about life not being worth
living. So, as with the others, we've found the best cure
is to send you back, to try harder, until you finally get
the point."

"Do we 'lukewarm idlers' often appear here, then?"

"More than anticipated. Some particularly
recalcitrant reprobates have been round the block a
few times before learning their lesson."

Before he could ask more questions, the demon,
along with Hell's gates, faded – just as those of Heaven
had done.

The next thing he knew, he was lying in hospital, feeling very groggy and in intense pain. A nurse was beside him tending his mid-section, which was swathed in bandages. "Like a mummy," to use Uncle's words. "Completely rigid."

"You're lucky to be alive," said the nurse. "Somehow the scythe managed to avoid your major organs."

Uncle then learnt what had happened to his earthly body in his absence. His neighbour, Walter, having witnessed the fall (he'd also been on high, up a ladder fixing his guttering), had immediately phoned for an ambulance. He'd then run round to my uncle's, expecting to find a corpse. The ambulance crew were similarly minded. It was only when they started swathing the scythe blade in blankets, having been careful to leave it in situ (it being too dangerous to remove), that Uncle emitted a few groans (fortunately, they'd managed to detach the blade from its wooden handle).

None of this, though, challenged Uncle Albert's conviction that, between his fall and recovery, he'd died and visited both Heaven and Hell. The only thing that shocked him was the fact that he'd returned to his old body, rather than coming back as he'd expected – thinking along Buddhist reincarnation lines – as a baby, to start over again. However, as he later reasoned, beginning from scratch would make him less likely to learn from his mistakes (if mistakes they were. Uncle remained unconvinced).

Realising the bizarre nature of his experiences, he largely kept them to himself, although he did fictionalise them in what became his first published novel and his most critically acclaimed book, *Extraterrestrial Trials*. It is this account that I've drawn on.

However far-fetched his experience might sound (his few confidants put it down to the anaesthetic), there was no doubting that Uncle was a changed man – even if not a reborn one. I can't say that I knew him well before the accident – I was only a teenager at the time – but even I could see a transformation.

So, too, did his would-be publishers, who now warmed to his works, just as he warmly and magnanimously accepted most of their suggested revisions. He even gave them a formal acknowledgement in *Extraterrestrial Trials*:

> My thanks to the various
> anonymous readers of earlier drafts
> of this work, without whom it
> would have been a different animal.
> My especial thanks to my editor,
> Gary Smyrna, for his patience and
> diligence, and not forgetting the
> salutary advice of St Peter and that
> anonymous demon.

Most people, of course, thought this last bit was just another of Uncle's little jokes.

Uncle's success continued to grow over the next two decades until he was in his late sixties, by which time he was the respected writer of five critically acclaimed novels. He'd even garnered a few literary prizes and become a regular at literary festivals. Towards the end of his life, he started putting in an occasional appearance on chat shows, too, coming across as affable and eccentric. But that all changed following an incident on *The Graham Norton Show* (Graham confessed to being a fan of Uncle's work, especially *Extraterrestrial Trials*).

Jan Caraway, a reality TV star and ex-drug addict who had found salvation in Christianity, was also on the show that night, promoting her memoirs. For some reason, Uncle Albert took exception to her, especially as he thought her memoir was ghost written by a hack of his acquaintance. Caraway's faith, he declared, had not saved her from diddly squat. She'd just swapped one drug for another. She might as readily have resorted to drugs to save her from an addiction to Christianity!

I think a clip from the show can still be found on YouTube. It caused a sensation at the time. Caraway, in turn, called Uncle "a callous atheist", a claim that he strongly rebutted, relating – for almost the first time in public – his personal meeting with St Peter. However, Uncle was quick to add that we shouldn't kow-tow to such arrogant beings. Those who have the audacity to label us, for eternity, as either sheep or goats! We should, said Uncle, refuse to play their childish games.

We should stand on our own two feet. You could see Graham Norton wishing that Albert was in the show's famous red chair, primed for ejection.

That was the last time Albert appeared on the media. A few articles surfaced in magazines, but there were no more novels. Uncle seemed to have reverted to his "pre-death" self. He disowned his published works, claiming that they were superficial, written to appease an audience that needed sweeteners to make their reality palatable. He said his earlier, unpublished works warranted more attention, in which he'd laid bare the barrenness of the human condition. Needless to say, his publishers were not impressed.

Shortly after this, it became known that Albert Palmerson had stomach cancer – a condition, it was stressed, that had nothing to do with his scythe accident. In a matter of months, he was dead. I was the only one present at the end. We'd become close, I like to think – as close as anyone could get to such an irascible character. It seems that I was one of the few who found his mordant humour engaging.

Uncle definitely didn't want a religious service – although, as he reiterated, he was no atheist. When I asked him about the fate of his remains, he suggested that we compost him. In the end, we interred him in a biodegradable casket. A few of his diehard fans were present, so we had some impromptu readings from his work – all, apart from my piece, taken from his published novels. As ever, the scene featuring the pearly/infernal gates was the most popular and made the burial quite uplifting, though I don't know what Albert would have made of it – or anyone else listening in!

Though Uncle had always been a sincere man, I too subscribed to the view that his other-worldly experience was more psychological than physical; that his encounter in the hereafter (or, in his case, the almost-after) could be explained in terms of the delusional effects of anaesthesia. I never let Uncle know my views, and I certainly still enjoyed fantasising about the fate of "lukewarm idlers" like himself.

Could, I wondered, writers like H.P. Lovecraft and Samuel Beckett have experienced similar rejections at those gates? Perhaps such rejections weren't their first, either. Perhaps decades before they'd originally approached those gates with the swagger of a Schopenhauer or a Nietzsche. How many mortal rounds, then, did it take before such rebels finally gave in and succumbed to writing happy-pappy books à la Billy Graham, Patience Strong and Barbara Cartland?

They were delightful reveries, though I could never picture Uncle Albert succumbing to such a Panglossian fate. As I said before, I think that, apart from his post-Grim Reaper period, he was always sincere. It was only that "reborn" self that was phony, with Uncle parodying the sort of good behaviour that the Immortals, sitting up in the gallery, might like to see.

I am also convinced that Uncle knew about his cancer before *The Graham Norton Show* and used it to "come out", to use a voguish term. But, unlike Job, Uncle refused to connive in that role as the pious, obsequious sufferer. By then, Uncle had had enough of playing the good guy. He, I'm sure, never intended to go gently into any good night.

He was more of William Blake's persuasion: "I must create a system or be enslaved by another man's; I will not reason and compare." And, I believe, he never did, having refused to vacate the naughty seat.

I like to imagine that Uncle Albert is still out there somewhere, still on the mortals' merry-go-round, orbiting through the decades.

As I said at the outset, I was inspired to put pen to paper (or, more accurately, finger to word processor) after reading an article in the *Sunday Times* entitled "A New Rimbaud", about the latest Wunderkind, Conrad Applebaum, a saturnine young poet (then aged only fifteen). Eagerly I examined that boy's picture, keen to see a family resemblance. There was no reason why there should be, but I did note that Uncle Albert had also died just over fifteen years before.

You're probably thinking that I too have lost it, like some QAnon fanatic who sees patterns of coincidence everywhere. Perhaps I am, but when I spotted the title of Applebaum's first volume of poems, I confess hot coffee landed in my lap: *Grim Reapings*, he'd called it. A coincidence, of course!

Loco Pete's Leap

L
ewis and Clark Caverns are up in the London
Hills of Montana. Though they are named for
those famous explorers, the two never made
it up here to discover this cave system. It's been over
three years since I was last here. But here I am again,
in the Visitors' Centre, waiting for the next tour to
begin. And, in preparation, I'm just recording these
few words. Bit of a farewell speech, really. Suicide note,
I guess you'd call it.

Yep, you heard me right. It's come to that.

Three years back, things were very different. Me and two friends, Bob Unger and Carl Stobart – all three of us postgrad alumni from Montana State Uni – had met up for a reunion, hoping to revisit old haunts, including our alma mater, and to discover some new ones. In our student days in Montana, we'd often gone hiking and climbing together.

A year on from our MBA, my two buddies had good jobs, unlike me, who'd taken a year out to travel, or "drift" as my parents described it. I'd fallen out of love with Business Studies, as my less than promising performance showed, and I wanted to do something different.

We'd just spent a day visiting Nevada City and Virginia City – now mere ghost towns, but once the richest gold spots in the old West – and were on our way to the Lewis and Clark Caverns. These expeditions were taking us to new territory.

The Caverns themselves are a great example of American ingenuity and enterprise. Rather than leave the cave system in its natural state, someone had blasted a whole new trail through the mountain, creating a gentle decline from top to bottom, complete with built-in steps to make it easy on the legs. The tour we'd signed up for, all those years ago, was a solid hour underground but, thanks chiefly to me, it took far longer.

Including our guide, Rusty, there were about fifteen of us on that tour. Rusty, as I recall, was an old-timer who'd lived in Montana most of his life and, like some nineteenth-century prospector with his pannings of gold, had hoarded every single anecdote he'd ever heard, just so's he could recycle them for our benefit. He particularly enjoyed regaling us with tales of Loco Pete, who'd become successful prospecting for gold in Nevada City.

Gold – doesn't that word just ring real pretty in your mouth?

Sorry. As I was saying, Rusty told us that this prospector was initially known as "Goldy" Pete, having had his first nuggets fashioned into a gleaming set of dentures. The nickname "Loco" only came later, after the ravages of drink and syphilis addled his brain.

Loco had come up to the caverns shortly after their discovery in the 1890s, hoping to discover more of the yellow stuff. He never did, even though his last words were, reputedly, "the motherload". Uttered, so Rusty informed us, as he plunged to his death in the cave's bowels.

Sure enough, there's a column of rock on "Loco Pete's Leap" – as it's known – that looks quite like a stooped old man with a long beard, about to topple. According to our trusty guide, Loco landed with a clang.

"R.I.P." said Rusty. "For you good folks, that's rest in pieces – gold pieces, of course."

The way the tour worked, Rusty would light our path through a particular section, turning on the electrics then switching them off as we moved to the next cavern.

There were, then, several times when we were plunged into complete darkness, often for dramatic effect. When this happened, the abrupt loss of light would create after-images, where clots of shadow seemed to move across our field of vision. It was something and nothing, but disarming nonetheless.

Coupled with this, the interconnected caverns amplified and distorted the everyday sounds of people clearing their throats, breathing heavily, shuffling their feet and so on. It was all too easy to imagine something uninvited lurking amongst us, especially as we regularly swapped positions on our way through the caverns. You were never quite sure where anyone in the group was. Was the check-shirted man ahead or behind you? Had the Japanese couple stopped to take a selfie? Had one of the old hiking guys bent to tie his lace?

As we approached a particularly narrow opening, I'd thought I was the one bringing up the rear. But, as I moved under the archway, something seemed to thump me on the back and I could sense a whispering at my ear. When we came to a wider section, I turned to see who was there, but saw no one. Just my shadow looming behind me. Beyond that, it was pitch black.

We were now in Sample Cavern where, so Rusty informed us, an older generation of tourists had been encouraged to take souvenirs of their visit, breaking off pieces of stalactite and hacking out bits of crystal. The damage was still there to see – as it would be for thousands of years to come.

I'd only been half-listening, though, preoccupied by what had thumped on my back. I must have been batting my hands around and reaching behind me, for the next thing I knew, there was Carl, imitating my actions, performing grotesque orangutan impressions for the amusement of others.

"Loco Pete rides again," declared Bob.

Rusty, picking up on my twitchiness, took this as his cue to launch into his trove of travellers' tales: anecdotes of explorers trapped underground and haunting the place; tales of the lingering spirits of Native Americans. He must have realised that I was slowing up the party with my twitchy behaviour, so was doing his best to keep everyone entertained. Soon he was talking about troglodytes, Bigfoot and the rest.

"Extraterrestrials coming soon," predicted Carl.

I won't prolong this account of my spelunking venture, but from that moment on I don't think I heard any more of Rusty's commentary. I was too preoccupied with what was clinging to my back. It seemed to be alive, breathing with a raspy, almost tinkling wheeze. It was getting heavier, too. It felt as though I had a rucksack on my back into which the rest of the party were lobbing stones, slowing my progress. I fell further and further behind. Rusty was a patient man, but I was obviously exhausting his store of anecdotes, let alone disrupting the tour schedule.

By the time we'd emerged from the cave system, I was on my knees – and I'd worn out everyone else. I could see that they were glad to be shot of me and my strange behaviour.

That, as I said, was three years ago. I'd like to tell you it was just a crazy day and I soon got over it. But that wasn't the case. That day, my life changed.

Bob and Carl left me to recuperate in the Visitor Centre while they sat outside in the truck, swigging beer. In the Centre, I discovered a copy of the *Financial Times*, left by some other visitor I guess. I hadn't seen a copy since my MBA, and I'd not opened it much then (as my tutors always complained). God knows why, but I picked it up and started reading about gold – *goldy-oldy-oldy* – trading. I became so absorbed that I didn't notice my buddies' return. It was only when Carl said, "He must be ill. Look what he's reading," that I registered their giggling presence.

What was especially weird was that I suddenly felt energised. No wheezing, no heavy limbs or bowed back. I felt better than I had for a long time, fired with a sense of purpose. I joined my friends in the truck and, uncharacteristically for me, refused the proffered beer. I wanted to hold on to my positive mindset, to keep a clear head, though perhaps clear is the wrong word, for clanking around in my skull, like a mantra, was the phrase, "Buy gold". In fact, I had to work hard at not proclaiming it aloud.

As I said before, this was all three years back, though today the Visitor Centre looks largely unchanged. I, on the other hand, am a very different man, as any of my friends – or former friends, I guess – would tell you.

On that distant day, I renounced travelling. At Bozeman airport, I saw off Bob and Carl before returning to Montana State Uni and seeking out Prof Garstang, one of my old tutors. I wanted his advice on … well, investing in gold, of course.

He couldn't believe it was me, one of his most disappointing students. However, I also knew that he'd had a soft spot for me, always believing I could do better. So, without any disapproving finger wagging, he ran with my enthusiasm and gave me a few tips and contacts.

On returning to New Jersey, I promptly invested what little savings I had in gold bullion.

Bullion, such a lovely word, ain't it? A Frenchie told me it came from his country. Bouillon being like a golden sauce, just like molten gold. Then you pour it into moulds to make those gold bars! Buy gold, buy gold, buy gold!

Apologies. That's my nemesis, Loco Pete. I thought the sedatives, washed down with camomile tea, might shut him up for a while, but he's coming round, obviously excited. I'll just take a couple more. It's a bit of an overdose, but what have I got to lose?

I have to say, all my hunches, gut reactions – call them what you will – come from him, his clanking dentures nibbling at my ears and proclaiming:

Buy more gold -old -old! Buy bullion -ion -ion!

Or:

Sell quick. Lighten your load -oad -oad!

There's always that metallic echo, as though we're still in those caves.

In material terms, I can't complain. I'm a success, someone to whom people look with new-found respect. My old Prof was particularly impressed, even though I'd quite spectacularly ignored his recent cautionary words. How did I always know, he'd asked, exactly when the market would peak and dip? And why did I not diversify into other commodities – platinum, tin, or silver? But, as I tried to explain, none of it had the appeal of the yellow stuff.

Goldy-oldy! Sing it loud! Let it run round your mouth like the water in your pan as you sift out the crap, leaving that gold to shine!

Apologies again. I've taken a break to let the sedatives take effect.

As I was saying, I had the Midas touch – as Prof Garstang put it – though it had its downside. Treating everyone as a commodity, I'd become a pariah. People shunned me. Friends first – even Bob and Carl – then family members and, finally, my wife, Christine. Yes, about two years ago, I got married.

I could, of course, have got hitched many times over, for women were forever flinging themselves at me, disgustingly rich and eligible as I was. Most, though, became quickly disillusioned. Not Christine. She was different, and tried in so many ways to help me, but eventually Loco Pete saw her off, too. She used to complain that I no longer kissed her but chewed on her lips as though assaying a coin. She too had become a commodity in my ceaseless hunt to "Buy gold!"

She might have put up with the nibbling, but not the obsessive pursuit of gold and the hard drinking that went with it. I'd like to say it was a way of escaping Loco Pete, but the more I indulged, the more like him I became – a bestial troglodyte, fit only to wander those Montana caverns. I'd even developed a stoop, as though to accommodate him, sitting up there between my shoulders, riding me like I was a pack animal.

I tried everything to escape his clutches. We relocated several times to different states before going abroad, initially to Europe then the Far East. Business colleagues thought I was diversifying, getting into the property market, but it was nothing so mercenary. I was simply trying to free myself from the clanking dentures and metallic voice of that crazy prospector.

Looking back, it was a ridiculous idea. As if I could escape the very thing that was riding me like a succubus, sucking the life out of me.

I saw doctors, but it's hard to be taken seriously – however rich you are – when you start to explain that you have this parasite, a loony old prospector called Loco Pete, who sits up between your shoulder blades and rides you like a mule. Mostly, they advised me to lay off the booze and prescribed tranquilisers. One specialist, who took my hunched posture seriously, did design a harness for me to wear. Loco Pete thought it a hoot. Just the thing to keep his pet burro in line!

The tranquilisers did help but, bit by bit, he was taking over. My thoughts, my posture, my obsessions – they were becoming his. I knew my mouth was not to be trusted, forever singing the praises of gold, apart from when it was being plain abusive. I'd even had my only gold filling removed, fed up with him forever probing it with his tongue – dammit, my tongue! Only my eyes, peaking out of their sockets like timid mice, felt like they were still my own.

So, perhaps you'll understand why I've decided to make my exit before Loco Pete possesses me completely. And, laying aside my own selfishness, it seems a duty to rid the world of his malevolent presence. A quick hop over the railings at Loco Pete's Leap and the man can re-enact his famous swan song.

I just need to send this recorded message to my lawyers. They already have a copy of my new will. Christine will be surprised, I think, to learn that most of my fortune is going to her, regardless of our formal separation. I've also tried to make my peace with other family members and old friends like Bob and Carl, all of whom should eventually hear this recording.

Sorry guys, but now you know the reason!

☾✲☽

Well, the above was to have been final but, as you can see, it turns out not to have been. It's now almost a year since I returned to the Lewis and Clark Caverns to end it all.

I did go on that tour, as planned. But, before I reached Loco Pete's Leap, I experienced a sudden sense of well-being, as though a great weight had been lifted from me. To be more explicit, I felt that lump on my back detach itself and disappear. Even in the restricted space of the caverns, I was suddenly walking taller.

And I've been a new man ever since. Even Christine and I are communicating again. As long as I don't mention one particular metal, everything's fine. Not that I have any wish to do so.

Apart, that is, from telling you about an interesting news item I saw the other day, about some whizz kid who made a killing trading … you know, trading the yellow stuff. I've often wondered whether he might have been on my last cavern trip. Should I get in touch? Should I warn him? Then I think of encountering Loco Pete again and decide not to. I couldn't bear to hear that clanking voice again.

I also wonder whether there might have been someone on my own first trip to the Lewis and Clark Caverns. Someone who'd also been intent on getting rid of Loco Pete. Someone who also, perhaps, came out a lighter, bouncier man.

I could probably look into that, too.

But I doubt I will.

Sláinte Peter, a *Fitzgerald's* man!

"Are youse lost?"

William and I had set off through the main streets of Dublin on a dry autumn evening, but somehow we'd left the crowds behind. We found ourselves alone, down a backstreet of semi-derelict properties. Though I'd always found Dublin a friendly city, this neighbourhood made me nervous. When we were certain there was no one around, we discreetly consulted our map. That's when this shortish, corpulent man confronted us. He seemed to have come from nowhere.

At the time, I was on my second annual trip to Dublin as an external examiner at Trinity. It was mid-November and William, my partner, had come along so we could turn the event into a mini break. On that first evening, before my official duties began the following morning, we were off for a pub supper. We'd been recommended The Mason's Apron as a bar that not only served food but also featured live music. However, despite directions, somewhere north of the Liffey we'd managed to get ourselves lost.

"We're looking for The Mason's Apron," William responded, "for a meal."

Despite the man's furtive appearance, he seemed to pose no threat. He had that helpful demeanour we'd so often encountered in Dublin.

"Never heard of it." He shook his head. "And haven't I lived here all my days?" He peered at our map. "Whereabouts is this Mason's Apron," he asked, before adding with a chuckle, "if not tied to the man hisself?"

It took us a second to appreciate his quip. We laughed politely. I pointed to the bar's location on the map, naming the street.

"Ah, John O'Connell's," he said. Bars in Ireland were often named after their landlords. "But they don't serve food."

I opened my mouth to disagree, then bit my tongue. He was the local after all. I was also aware that he was already dancing off ahead of us.

"I'll show youse where you'll enjoy a bite. Just around the corner."

We found ourselves chasing after him as William said, "There's no need. Directions will be fine."

"It's a pleasure, to be sure. And," he patted his paunch, "this fella could do with the exercise."

For all his rotundity, the man moved with surprising agility. We found it an effort to keep up. He was like a character from Tourism Ireland, wearing a rather old-fashioned brown jacket over a jersey, grey trousers, stout black brogues, flat cap and muffler. Despite his breathless speed, he also kept up a monologue detailing the exploits of other Dublin characters. I particularly remember him telling us about a tobacconist who kept a goat in his backyard.

"One day," our guide said, "it escaped and climbed on a bus. And would you credit it?" He turned on his heel to face us, halting for the first time in some ten minutes. "Wasn't it the very bus that goes to Smithfield Fruit and Vegetable Market?"

While he stood there laughing, cradling his quivering belly, we asked him how much further we had to go. We could already see the Liffey in the distance and were worried we'd end up back at our hotel.

"Just a few steps so," he promised, once again prancing ahead. He hurried us past a few attractive-looking bars with food boards propped outside. "Ah – no, no," he'd say dismissively.

Finally, he halted outside a less prepossessing building and proclaimed, "Fitzgerald's!"

He ushered us in. Like so many Dublin bars it had a narrow frontage but reached back cavernously. He threaded us through to the rear, where there was an eating area. On the way, he hailed a few people – clearly this was his local – but we both had the feeling that he wasn't as well-known as he seemed to think himself.

We presumed that, at the very least, the man would want a pint for his troubles. But he declined, fondling his paunch. "Sad to say, but this ole fella can't handle it any more."

We'd assumed we'd get to know him better – we had quite an affection for him – but all we learnt, aside from the fact that he used to work on the railways at Connolly Station, was his name.

"If you want to show your gratitude, just raise a glass to Peter, a Fitzgerald's man." With that, he turned and left. Not even a handshake.

Fitzgerald's menu was quite restricted: Irish stew, coddle, or fish and chips. By this time, though, we were ravenous and didn't care. And, despite our misgivings, we thoroughly enjoyed our supper of battered cod, amusing ourselves rehearsing Peter's anecdotes, imagining our friends enjoying them at some time in the future.

Even then, the night wasn't over. As we sat, savouring a coffee and a Jameson's, some young musicians wandered in and started to play, using the premises to rehearse. It was a rare treat, especially when they launched into a tune called "The Mason's Apron". It reminded us to raise our glasses to Peter. Thanks to him, we'd ended up only a few minutes from our hotel bed.

As we were paying our bill, we asked the landlord whether he knew The Mason's Apron and if it did meals. He confirmed that it did. Everyone knew about that particular pub, he informed us, for, "back in the day, wasn't it blown to bits? John O'Connell's it then was, but it quickly changed its name."

The following day was the exam board, so I had my work cut out. I left William to enjoy being a tourist. I might have known though, being a historian, he'd skipped the hotspots and made straight for the National Library, where he'd gone through the newspaper archives, looking for information about John O'Connell's.

That evening, on the plane back to England, William showed me some of the photocopies he'd made. The bar had experienced bomb damage back in 1983, killing three and injuring many more. As we'd never made it to this mythical bar, it all seemed academic to me, but then William thrust another cutting under my nose – one he'd been holding back.

I was confronted with a black-and-white photo of a portly man who, even in the grainy reproduction, was immediately recognisable as our Dublin guide. The caption confirmed it – "The late Peter Ryan, father of four, platform attendant at Connolly" – except that he'd been anything but "late" when we'd encountered him. It was then that William began humming *The Twilight Zone* theme and the hair on my scalp began to bristle.

I went back through William's cuttings, then, reading them more carefully. Peter, we learnt, was one of the three fatalities. "Wrong place, wrong time," was the sub-heading of the section discussing him. In it, the landlord of Fitzgerald's – where else? – was quoted as saying: "I don't know what Peter was doing in O'Connell's that night. He was a fierce Fitzgerald's man." With a touch of gallows humour, the landlord went on to warn regulars about flirting with other bars. The piece ended by saying that the locals there had raised a glass to Peter, "one of the boys."

We were dumbfounded. I reminded William of Peter's precise words.

"He said he'd lived in Dublin all his days. Past tense!"

"And he asked to be remembered as a Fitzgerald's man," replied William.

I don't think anyone believes in ghosts until they meet one. Even then you might not know it's a ghost. It was from then on that William and I became convinced that ghosts moved amongst us, though neither the living nor the dead could be sure who was who.

❨✹❩

The following November, I was booked to return to Dublin for my final stint as an external. I had intended to go on my own, but William was keen to visit the now mythical Mason's Apron. He reasoned that it would give more verisimilitude to our story, though we'd already dined out on it for almost a year.

The bar of The Mason's Apron had obviously been modified – essential after that explosion back in the eighties – but it still felt authentic and cosy. There was live music, as we'd been promised. Fiddles, banjos, guitars and bodhrans clamoured for attention at the far end.

We sat close to the door so we could hear ourselves speak. Round the walls were framed newspaper cuttings, detailing the pub's fate. Most were familiar from William's research, but there were also some more recent ones, with colour photographs.

The first showed a car's nose buried in the brickwork of the bar's frontage. "Jinxed bar?" queried the headline. We read about some joyriding youths, hotly pursued by the garda, who had ploughed into the pub, killing two of the vehicle's occupants and injuring many inside the bar itself.

As I read through the piece, I became aware of William urgently shaking my arm. "What date was it that we ended up at Fitzgerald's?"

With the minutes from last year's examiners' meeting freshly in mind, I told him that the day before had been the twelfth of November. As I said it, William pointed to the date on the cutting – the thirteenth – the day after the accident.

More spookily, the time of the accident was also mentioned: seven o'clock at night. It took us a few minutes to reconstruct our movements of a year ago. With eyes wide, we realised we'd been on our way to this unlucky bar shortly before seven, and … if it hadn't been for Peter, we'd probably have made it in time for a very different rendezvous.

We both felt an irrational need to move towards the musicians at the rear of the bar. Once there, and having ordered our meal, what could we do but raise a glass to our ghostly saviour, "Sláinte Peter, a Fitzgerald's man!"

A Hint of Complicity

ike Ansom couldn't keep his eyes open any longer. He would have to take a nap. He swung his white Ford Sierra into a lay-by and eased the car to a standstill. Prising his hands from the steering wheel, he massaged his aching neck. This really was a young man's game, he told himself.

He also needed a pee but was so tired he couldn't summon the energy to go for one. He kept nodding off, then coming round with a painful jerk as his head lolled onto his chest. Finally, he managed to open the car door and ease himself out of his claustrophobic cockpit. "I'm too old for this," he reiterated, but retirement was still a way off. He tried to arch his back, bracing his hands against his hips for leverage, but his hands kept sliding off the rolls of excess flesh. He staggered into the undergrowth. Fortunately, the lay-by was deserted.

Within minutes he was back in his car, settling himself into his seat. He struggled to adjust it to the reclining position, but eventually gave up. His sample books of fabrics, filling the back seat and footwell, wouldn't budge. He really should get them organised, he told himself once again. In the end, he fell asleep with the seat partially reclined, too exhausted to do more.

Unfortunately for Mike, even sleep didn't bring peace. He had one of those dreams where you think you are still awake, wondering why sleep won't come. In the course of this waking dream, he'd looked up to see, at the end of the lay-by, a girl hitching. A very attractive girl, too, with blonde hair tied in bunches, wearing blue dungarees and a denim jacket. The sight of her made him abandon any attempt at slumber (so he thought). He would give this young woman a lift. It was dangerous, he told himself, for girls to be out on their own. He always worried about them, picturing his own daughter in a similar predicament.

The girl gratefully accepted a lift and they drove off. Although he kept the conversation light and playful, he found himself aroused by the young woman's presence. He could feel his penis harden in his trousers, constricting them further. Even turning the steering wheel was difficult. And the motion of the car was only making matters worse. He groaned, then, on impulse, found himself unzipping and pulling her head down towards his groin and then, and then …

He woke with a jerk, alone in his car, an uncomfortable stickiness at his crotch. He was still in the lay-by. Although it had only been a dream, he felt unclean, disgusted. Fortunately, the lay-by remained quiet, and he managed to clean himself up without attracting attention.

Feeling more human again, Mike started the engine and gently pulled away, checking his rear-view mirror. What a day! He couldn't wait to get home. Then, as his eyes focused on the road ahead, he spotted, standing on the grass verge, that self-same girl he'd dreamt about: large blue eyes, blonde hair in bunches, dungarees.

He felt so disgusted with himself, let alone appalled at the untrustworthiness of his unconscious mind, that he was tempted to drive straight past. But he knew he couldn't leave her there. In fact, he wondered how she could have got there in the first place. It was a dual carriageway. There were no other routes apart from the one he was taking.

He drew alongside and opened the passenger door, experiencing an eerie feeling of déjà vu. Was he, once again, mouthing the very words he'd used in his dream? His sense of mortification tormented him. But there she was, beside him in the car, thanking him profusely for rescuing her. She closed the door and they moved onto the main carriageway.

His main concern was that the car might smell. The dusty fabric samplers were bad enough, but what about his personal aroma? Could she have spotted him, in the lay-by, when he'd been, er ... asleep? Had it looked like he'd been ... playing with himself? Even in his mind, he couldn't countenance the word masturbating. He felt sick and swallowed hard.

The young woman showed no signs of distaste, however, and they soon settled into a relaxed conversation after she'd expressed an interest in his fabric samples. Sam (short for Samantha) was a textiles student. He was delighted to see her so captivated by the patterns and textures in his books. He, too, had always found them a great source of comfort: dependable and predictable in their orderliness. Sam asked permission to take some sketches and Mike was delighted to watch her copy some designs into her pink-and-white, polka-dot notebook.

Eventually, he dropped her off at the end of the street where she had her digs. It was slightly out of his way but, as he told her, he didn't like to see girls hitching on their own. He worried for their safety, especially after his lurid dream.

He would have driven her right to her door, but she insisted that the end of the road was fine. And he realised that, were he to be more assertive, that in itself might sound creepy. Even so, he carefully watched her walk down the road until she turned into a gateway.

It wasn't until he was on the ring road going out of town that he noticed the polka-dot notebook wedged beside the passenger seat.

At the next roundabout he started to retrace his steps. It was getting dark now. But, crawling down her street, he thought he could remember where she'd turned in. He parked his car and went to the door. He had thought of posting her book through the letter box, but it was too bulky and, besides, he wanted to make sure he had the right place. If he were honest, he also had to admit that he was looking forward to seeing her bright young face again. At the end of his long and weary day, she had been a breath of fresh air.

Eventually, the door opened and an elderly woman stood before him. He'd expected someone younger: a student of some sort. He started to explain himself, then abandoned the attempt, asking more directly, "Can I speak to Sam?"

As he said her name, it was as though he had struck the woman. The colour drained from her face and she started to tremble. As delicately as he could, he took her arm, fearing she might collapse, and he called out for help.

An older man appeared, his face creased in anger. He obviously thought Mike had attacked her. She quickly regained her composure and reassured her husband she was alright. Both of them now seemed keen to invite Mike inside.

It certainly did not look like a student house. Had Sam deceived him? Mike wondered. Had she only pretended to enter this house? But that still didn't account for this older woman's reaction. The name Sam had triggered something.

And then it all came out. Mr and Mrs Benson used to rent rooms to girls at the art college, but they had stopped doing so some fourteen years ago, after Sam's tragic death.

When Mr Benson announced this, Mike stopped him, waving Sam's polka-dot notebook in the air as he related his earlier encounter with her. Were the couple suffering some form of dementia, he wondered.

Mr Benson went across to a bureau and extracted a book of cuttings, which he passed to Mike, who scanned the yellowing rectangles of newspaper. They came adrift as he read them, the Sellotape brittle and discoloured. There she was, right enough: blond hair tied in bunches, just as he'd seen her. Mike read the caption: "Bright, blue-eyed Sam Rowlandson, just 18."

Mrs Benson leaned across and touched his arm. "You're not the first," she said. "We understand."

Mr Benson was on his feet again. "This," he said, waving a long woollen scarf before Mike's eyes, "was dropped off by someone else, five years ago. Also left in the car when she got out."

"We think it's the tip of the iceberg," said Mrs Benson, "but most drivers wouldn't have known where she lived."

"What about her parents? Do they know about this?" asked Mike.

"They don't," said Mr Benson. "Both dead, hearts broken."

Mike looked down at Sam's notebook, still lying on the chair arm beside him: a tangible, physical object.

"We hadn't heard anything since the ten-year anniversary of her murder," said Mr Benson. "We thought that might be it."

"And then you come along," added his wife. "Let's get you a cuppa." Her voice choked. She left the room, her husband following soon after.

Mike took the time to read the cutting he'd been holding, the one with her familiar picture on. "Girl Hitcher Murdered!" announced the headline. According to the report, she'd never left the lay-by. She and her boyfriend had had a row, it said, and he'd driven off, abandoning her there. Twenty minutes down the road, he'd calmed down, turned the car round and gone back, but couldn't find her. He assumed she'd accepted a lift. As was later discovered, though, she'd never made it back to the Bensons' or, indeed, to her parents' house.

Within the week, her body had been discovered in the lay-by undergrowth, half buried. The boyfriend, a fellow art student, had initially been charged, but DNA tests on the semen lodged in her throat – she'd choked – had cleared him. The murderer had never been found, so a later cutting – a decade on – informed Mike.

Mike drank his tea, though it almost choked him, and thanked the Bensons. He left the notebook with them. It seemed right, somehow, that Sam's belongings be kept together – those tangible artefacts that, bizarrely, completed the journey she never had. He knew he had quite enough to remember her by.

As the Bensons closed the door behind him, Mike was overpowered at the thought of what Sam had experienced. Some smelly torso thrusting itself at her, suffocating her, a gush of claggy seed filling her throat. Mike barely reached the front gate before the vomit exploded from him. For the second time that day he had to clean himself up.

As he stumbled back to his Sierra, Mike tried desperately to hold on to this feeling of empathy with Sam. The alternative was too unthinkable: that he might have more in common with her killer; someone into whose skin he had so readily slipped.

Mike fumbled with the car keys, eventually resettling himself into the womb of his Sierra. He sat there for some time, distracted. Finally, he reached for one of his fabric books and opened it across his lap. Mechanically, he flipped through the samples, desperately trying to focus on the designs; seeking succour in their dependable patterns – patterns that had, until this particular evening, always offered him solace, given his life some sort of shape and meaning.

RIP

"To think, one day I'll be joining them," said Mum, at the funeral of one of her many aunts. It freaked out me and Kate, my sister. But Mum didn't seem upset, like it would be a happy reunion or something. Looking around, Cranbury churchyard was certainly full of Walkers.

"We ought to get some sort of group discount," Kate whispered to me.

The reception was held at Aunt Agatha's as she had the biggest garden. After a couple of hours, Kate and I had had enough, so we went to explore the village. We hadn't been there for ages. We meandered round for about an hour before we made our way back, cutting through the churchyard.

We were like young kids again, letting off steam, running about and leaping out at each other. Of course, Aunt Agatha's sherry might have made us more silly than usual. At fifteen, Kate should have known better. I was only thirteen, so had an excuse.

I'd been hiding behind a particularly impressive tomb. It was like a big chest freezer carved out of stone, with a figure lying on top. "Recumbent," as Kate informed me. The side of the tomb where I was crouching was pressed hard against a yew tree. It smelt a bit disgusting, but I could put up with it until Kate found me. I could see some carvings on it. Diddy demonic figures with toasting forks, chasing serpents. There was also some carved writing, which I could only just make out by tracing the letters with my finger. The words weren't English and spelt out, "Eadem mutata resurgam".

It made no sense, though "mutata" sounded familiar. There was that annoyingly catchy song from *The Lion King*, "Hakuna Matata", which we had to sing in school. All about being cool and laid back. For someone "recumbent" in a chest freezer, it sounded about right!

Just then, I heard Kate yelling. She'd given up searching. I'd had enough of my smelly hiding place anyway, so, pushing the branches aside, I came round to the sunnier side of the tomb, nearer the path.

"Thought you'd joined our relatives," said Kate, milking our standard joke. "Been getting to know," she read the name off the tomb, "Ambrose Jeremiah Walker, 1796–1849, have we? Must be one of Mum's oldest relatives. Never heard of him before."

I turned to show Kate the cavorting little devils, but there were none on this side. Just a rather clumsy angel on one knee, carrying a shield. I asked her about the phrase on the other side: "Eadem mutata resurgam."

"No idea," she said.

"I thought you did languages."

"Not dead ones."

"What's a dead language when it's at home? One spoken by corpses?"

"No, stupid! Latin and Greek. Like this one." She pointed to the phrase inscribed on the angel's shield: "Requiescat in Pace."

"What's that about, then?"

Before she could answer, the vicar, who'd officiated at the burial, went past, "You perhaps know it better in English," he said. "Rest in Peace. R.I.P."

"Oh, yeah," I smiled, feeling like a simpleton. "What about the words on the dark side?"

"I didn't know there were any," he replied in his fruity voice.

"Yeah. 'Eadem mutata resurgam'," I said.

"That would mean, something like, I shall rise again, the same but changed," he intoned as he walked away.

I waited till he was out of earshot. "Old Ambrose would certainly need to get changed after all that time among the maggots and worms!" I began waving my arms in the air, mock attacking Kate.

Walking back to the reception, that earworm of a Disney tune was tunnelling its way through my head. I began singing it to the words on the tomb.

"You sound weird," said Kate. "Are you trying to imitate that plummy-voiced vicar?"

"I used to have a plum in my mouth," I said, "but those stinky worms snaffled it."

We stayed at the reception until quite late and drank more of Aunt Agatha's sherry. Mum was enjoying a catch-up with her relatives. Even so, Kate and I did manage to ask about Ambrose Jeremiah.

"We don't usually talk about him," Aunt Agatha confided. "Bit of a black sheep."

She told us that he'd once been the vicar in Cranbury but had then gone off to Africa as a missionary. "He returned a changed man," she said. "Lost his faith and developed some strange ideas. He was branded a heretic and I don't think he'd have been buried in the churchyard but for his brother, Simon, who'd given a lot of money to the parish. That tomb of his," she concluded, "was particularly contentious. He'd designed it himself."

✹

Having dispatched the last of the relatives, we cleared up and eventually went to bed. Aunt Agatha was putting us up. I thought I'd sleep like a log after all the food and sherry. But I didn't. I dreamt about Ambrose Jeremiah. One of those weird dreams where you don't realise you're asleep.

In the dream, Ambrose has risen from his grave and walks all the way down to Aunt Agatha's. He shuffles up the stairs and into my room. Talk about nightmares! He pushes open the door and, in best zombie style, clatters in, all stiff and scarecrow-like. There's worms and maggots dripping from his nose, like bogies, and crawling through his hair, too. Gross!

But there's worse. He makes his way over to my bed and, as if I'm not there, sits on the edge, then swings round his legs and climbs in. Aaargghh! I couldn't even move. It was one of those dreams where your legs won't work and your tongue's superglued to the roof of your mouth.

I woke in a right sweat. Worst part was, after I'd finally recovered, I dreamt about him again. I didn't share any of this with Kate or Mum. But the following morning I must have looked shot at. Mum noticed immediately, especially as I seemed to have lost my appetite. She asked if anything was wrong.

I did have a bit of a sore throat, which was painful when I swallowed. It made my voice sound strange.

"It's that plummy worm again," joked Kate.

"Really!" said Mum.

Normally, I'd have laughed, but the memory of Ambrose's leering face froze me.

☾✦☽

When we got back home, about three hours away, I went straight to bed. I still felt lousy and my throat was swollen. I slept, but erratically, for disgusting old Ambrose kept appearing. It was as if he'd hitched a ride.

The dreams went on, night after night. Revolting! Ambrose, dragging his Worzel Gummidge bones into my room and clambering into bed alongside me, as though he belonged there. He stank of muck and decay, but that didn't bother him. He just pushed himself up against me. I could feel his scrawny frame – knobbly knees and scraggy hips – hard against my back. Even though he'd been dead for centuries, he felt solid enough.

At first, I woke every time he started pushing against me. Was I going to be, well, assaulted … raped? Not just by a dirty old man, either, but a dirty *deceased* old man – possibly *diseased*, too. It was too gross to contemplate. After several nights, though, the dreams no longer woke me. I think I'd realised he wasn't actually going to "penetrate" me or anything disgusting like that, despite the repulsive grunts and groans close to my ear. It was more as though he was trying to invade me, to squeeze his body into mine.

It was not something I could share with Mum or Kate, either, although I did ask my sister whether she'd had any weird dreams since our return from Cranbury. All I got was a blank look. Not that I'd wish bog-breath on anybody else.

If I could've pointed to some physical evidence, it might have been different. A few straggly white hairs of his, perhaps, or some scaly skin. But no. No one noticed anything. It was strictly between him and me.

I tried everything to shake him off. I moved my bed across the room, then started sleeping in the spare bedroom. Finally, I decamped to the settee downstairs. Mum thought I was nuts. It didn't work anyway. And why would it? He'd already followed me all the way from Cranbury. What difference would a change of room make?

Eventually, Mum took me to the doctor. My neck glands remained swollen and I still had that strange, plummy twang to my voice. The doctor, though, could find little wrong. He put it down to puberty. My voice was breaking, he said, and I ought to try and relax till it settled down. I certainly yodelled a fair bit.

"Quite sexy," said Mum, to cheer me up.

Kate said it sounded as though I'd taken elocution classes. It definitely impressed Miss Waters, our English teacher, who persuaded me to join the drama society.

"There's hardly any boys in it," she added, tipping me a wink.

Then other things started happening. My sore throat got better, but it still felt constricted, as though clogged with phlegm. Our doctor got me an appointment with a specialist. But I knew there was more to it than any throat specialist could sort. The muscles of my tongue and mouth would contort themselves in strange ways and, occasionally, I'd blurt out something insulting: "Harlot!" "Blackamoor!" "Nance!" Fortunately, most of these insults were so old-fashioned (I'd had to look them up) that no one took exception. I tried to disguise them with sudden coughing fits, too. It was exhausting, though. Schoolfriends must have thought I had Tourette's or something.

Then my outbursts got more serious. It first happened in a class debate. I not only shouted down Avril Saunders but then I disrespected her. In fact, women in general. I told Avril she should know her place; that it was her duty to defer to her superiors, like me! Fortunately, the class laughed. They thought I was being ironic, especially as I said it in that extra-posh voice. But I could tell that many in the class felt intimidated. I apologised to Avril straightaway.

I tried to guard against these outbursts, but it's hard to monitor yourself when you don't know what's coming next. Sexist, racist, xenophobic, homophobic – you name it, I was there. People began keeping their distance – apart from some English Defence League lads, who suddenly befriended me!

Kate and Mum were really concerned. In fact, I caught Kate going through my search history. She must have thought I was being radicalised or something. Ambros-ised, more like.

I kept my jaws clamped after that, which made me even more anti-social. The throat specialist said I had "elective mutism" and referred me to a psychologist who diagnosed "dissociative episodes". He tried to identify some event that had been traumatic, initially homing in on Dad's departure. And when that didn't fit (the dates were wrong), he suggested that I might have been closer to my recently deceased Aunt Matilda than I'd realised.

By this point I was on the verge of giving in to Ambrose. I'd been prescribed some heavy-duty tranquilisers and I kept to my room, even taking my meals there. Ambrose, I could feel, was getting stronger, cockier.

Then it dawned on me that it wasn't enough to try and suppress him. The effort was draining me, making me more susceptible to his control. I needed to exorcise him in some way. I needed something like a Harry Potter expel-Ambrosius spell, before he expelled me!

☾✳☽

Things came to a head when Mum lost another of her aunts. Aunt Agatha. Our favourite, I guess.

Whenever we went back to Mum's village, it was with her that we used to stay. Her death came out of the blue, even though she was in her eighties.

Once again, we set off for Cranbury. But this time we stayed at the village pub as Aunt Agatha's house was already up for sale. Mum was really upset and, I guess, very concerned about taking me along. She and Kate were quite aware of the embarrassment I could cause, but I'm so pleased they risked it. Not, I guess, that they really had much option. I don't think I could have been left on my own.

The funeral went without mishap. I was quite relaxed amongst Mum's relatives, always a jolly lot. This time I got talking to Aunt Judy, the youngest of the three aunts. Remembering that I'd been enquiring last time, she volunteered a bit more information about Ambrose.

According to her, Ambrose had attempted to found a new religion. Something about an elect few being reincarnated at some future time, returning to rule the world, overthrowing Christianity and other belief systems. It sounded bizarre and we all laughed, though the noise I made came out more like a wheeze as I felt my throat constricting, courtesy of … guess who?

Aunt Judy also told me more about Ambrose's tomb. Originally, it had been designed with the devilish figures running all round it. However, the church had refused to allow such a monstrosity. A new stonemason was engaged. He chipped away the devilish ornamentation from the side on show, replacing it with the kneeling angel. At the insistence of the then vicar, the more lurid side was hidden from sight, and he oversaw the planting of a yew tree to conceal it more thoroughly.

Aunt Judy cheered me up more than I could have hoped. It wasn't so much what she was saying as the effect I could feel her words having on my "guest". Until this point, Ambrose had been relatively quiet, but I could sense his mounting anger and resentment. Fortunately, thanks to my former dealings with him, I had become more skilled in Ambrose management.

Kate, who'd been alongside me listening to all this (she was my minder), suggested that we return to the graveyard and take another look at his tomb. Before hearing Aunt Judy, it would have been my worst nightmare but, sensing Ambrose's reluctance, I was energised. If *he* didn't want to go there, *I* most certainly did.

Kate and I set off for the churchyard. The closer we came, the more I could sense Ambrose backpedalling. He attempted to immobilise my legs, then abruptly released them, almost causing me to sprawl headlong. He then switched his attack. Suddenly, I had to deal with a mouthful of vitriol spewing from my lips. Fortunately, I knew Ambrose's ways by now. My elective mutism prevailed.

We made it to the churchyard. Kate said she wanted to see the "dark side". I'd have been happy for her to do so but for the fact that Ambrose felt likewise. I stepped in front of Kate, blocking her path. I should have said something but my mute guard was still up. Seeing the state I was in, she readily complied.

Why was Ambrose so keen for Kate to see the dark side? Did he hope to ensnare her, too? Or was Ambrose intending to jump ship, from me to her? Or did he simply want to prevent us from taking the main path? I remembered Aunt Judy's words about the alterations to this side of his tomb, where Ambrose's devils had been replaced by the kneeling angel.

As I steered us down the main path, Ambrose's displeasure increased. I felt his bony fingers nipping at my tongue like pincers. Once again, he'd involuntarily given me a sign.

The nearer we came, the more my tongue, like a trapped eel, writhed to be free. I feigned submission until the inscription was in view. Then I shouted out those Latin words, "Requiescat in Pace".

The adrenalin rush was instant. It felt like I'd puked up something disgusting. I even looked around for the mess. Nothing, except for a heady feeling of release.

"There's no need to shout," Kate was saying. I apologised. "Your voice," she said. "It's like it used to be."

I barely heard her. The ground was rising towards me. Kate must have thought I was having a fit of some sort. But I'd never felt better and, after a moment's unconsciousness (so Kate later told me), I was on my feet again.

Kate was eager to get me back to the reception. First, though, I had something else to do. To her disgust, I grabbed handfuls of soil from a nearby mound, no doubt awaiting someone else's interment. Round the back of Ambrose's tomb, I smeared the earth into the grooved letters. Though I wasn't aware at the time, Kate tells me I started singing "Hakuna Matata", but this time sticking to the original words.

"One day," I told Kate as I re-emerged, clarted with mud, "I'll come back with a chisel and do the job properly."

She didn't know what I was on about, but she did know that it was the old me talking. We linked arms and, to the bewilderment of any villagers we encountered, gave that Disney song a truly anthemic outing.

Falling Fast?

As Veronica's car reversed out of the driveway, Andrew looked fondly at his house. His freshly varnished front door – would he ever see it again? Would he ever again need his front-door key? He was grateful that his younger sister was preoccupied with reversing. She couldn't see the tears puddling his eyes.

It had been a bad year. First, he'd lost his wife, Doris, after years of progressively debilitating MS; then his best pal, Len, a friend since primary school, had succumbed to a virulent prostate cancer. And now, here was he, about to have an operation to remove a tumour from his bowel.

Veronica, herself a nurse, had assured him that his own treatment was straightforward, but he was unconvinced. And, after she'd shown him a stoma bag, explaining its function and how it would be attached, he'd been utterly despondent.

Mournfully, as Veronica accelerated away, Andrew watched his front door slide from view. While she drove, Andrew opened the letter that had clattered onto the mat just before the two of them had left home. As Andrew had suspected, it was from Len's brother, Walter. This was the fourth such letter he'd received concerning Len's remains.

Andrew had been executor of his friend's will and, in accordance with Len's wishes, he'd had Len's body cremated. Walter, though, had not been happy, and was even less so when Andrew had taken possession of the ashes with a view to having them scattered. Walter had demanded that his brother's ashes be returned, so they might be "buried properly".

It had caused Andrew much heartache, but he was resolute that he should honour his friend's dying request. The problem was, Len had never specified where he'd like his ashes scattered, so, for the last four months, his remains had nestled in a casket under Andrew's bed. Had other events not intervened, Andrew was convinced he would have done something by now, as he'd frequently told Veronica.

"The usual demand, is it?" asked his sister, nodding towards the letter. "You don't think, while we're out, he'll try to burgle us?"

"Bugle us?" asked Andrew, perplexed.

Veronica looked exasperated. "You're getting deafer. No, Andrew, not *The Last Post*. You're not on your way out! I said *burgle*. Steal Len's ashes."

They laughed. It lightened the mood as they made their way to the James Cook Hospital in Middlesbrough.

☾✹☽

"See," said Veronica as, a week later, she nosed her car back into the driveway. "All safe and sound."

Andrew was overjoyed to see his house again. As they sat alongside each other in the car, preparing themselves for the ordeal of getting him inside, Andrew told his sister about the masked figure in the operating theatre who'd approached him with a felt tip, marking him up for "external plumbing". Andrew confessed that, at first, he'd thought the man had said "pummelling". That made her chuckle, which gave him the courage to tell her about what had happened next.

"I feared the worst and, as I was going under, I prayed to be spared a stoma. Next thing I know, I'm looking up and there's Len hovering over me, telling me about his prostate operation. He kept saying that he'd known, at the time, that he was not long for this world. 'Falling fast,' he told me, speaking in that broad Yorkshire accent of his. But then he told me that I'd be alright. 'All will be well,' he'd said, and pointed behind him to a beautiful beck with a waterfall in the distance. I could see it, clear as day. We were both playing there, children once again, paddling in the water.'"

Andrew was pleased to observe that Veronica took his experience seriously, though she did make the point that, following an anaesthetic, vivid dreams – delusions even – were quite common. They then summoned the energy to manhandle Andrew out of the car to his front door, where Victoria ceremonially passed him his key. He managed to turn the lock, but still needed help pushing the door ajar.

Andrew was embarrassed at how dependent on his sister he was. He was aware that she'd put her own life on hold for him. Before his illness, too, she'd looked after Doris, effectively being her full-time carer during those last gruelling months. Looking back, Andrew was ashamed of how he'd used his sister, feebly excusing himself on the pretext that he, personally, couldn't deal with illness. He now knew better.

The following morning, Veronica showed Andrew the decluttering she'd initiated. It was time, she said, for each of them to begin a new life, liberating themselves from the lumber they'd inherited after clearing their parents' house. Andrew, though, was not really paying attention. He was arrested by the sight of just one object – Len's casket – which Veronica had retrieved from under Andrew's bed. It was a stark reminder that his friend's ashes still needed dealing with.

Len's words from the operating theatre reverberated in his head, and Andrew suddenly saw them in a different light. What if Len had been telling him that he, Andrew, was now "falling fast"? That when Len had said, "All will be well," he was thinking of the afterlife, where the two of them would forever be playing by some Edenic stream?

"Are you alright?" Veronica asked, cutting through his reverie.

Later that evening, Veronica came to tuck him up in bed, making him aware of the bell on his bedside table. As children, their mother had always put that bell by their bedsides when they were sick. It brought tears to Andrew's eyes as he lay there thinking how lucky he'd been to have had Veronica diagnose his condition so early, and to have her frogmarch him down to A&E. Unlike, that is, poor Len, who'd had no one close enough to spot his cancer.

On the final night of her intended stay, Veronica was woken by Andrew's cries. She discovered him feverish, his abdominal wound suppurating. As for Andrew himself, he was oblivious. In his delirium, he thought it was Len who'd come to his side.

"Falling fast," his friend was once more saying to him, as Andrew felt bony fingers poking at his wound.

Then he realised that it was not Len but Veronica. "It's alright, Andrew," she was saying. "Just an infection."

"But am I falling fast?" asked Andrew. "Am I going downhill?"

"Course not! But we do need to get you back to A&E."

☾✻☽

It was almost dawn before Andrew was attended to. He couldn't believe how many others had found themselves in crisis that night.

As his dressing was removed, all he could see was what looked like a giant zip fastener reaching from his navel to his groin. It was a line of metal staples. Then Andrew noticed the liquid leaking from his wound. The doctor said he'd have to be readmitted and put on an intravenous antibiotic. However, as there were no beds available, Andrew was finally prescribed tablets and allowed home.

"A shame they couldn't take you in. Just in case," said Veronica on the way back. "Still, you've got me, haven't you?"

"What have I got?" asked Andrew, deaf as ever.

☾✻☽

A week later, Veronica voiced her concerns to her friend Jenny, a district nurse, who confirmed Veronica's suspicions. Andrew could hear them chatting, though their words — *dehiscence*, *fascia*, *debridement* — were meaningless to him. However, Andrew was now convinced that Len's prediction — that he was falling fast — was coming true.

In Andrew's eyes, this prognosis was confirmed when he found himself back in Surgical Outpatients, being prepped for a second anaesthetic. It was explained that his wound would be re-opened and the infected tissue removed. What no one had prepared him for, though, was another encounter with Len.

"Falling fast, lad," Len pronounced once more. "As I keep telling thee. When will tha' heed me, lad?"

❰✸❱

Back home, Veronica nursed Andrew assiduously. As she confided to Jenny, she was increasingly worried about her brother, "not physically, but his mindset." She told Jenny about Andrew's delusions, the "visits" from his late friend, supposedly predicting Andrew's demise. "*Falling fast,*" repeated Veronica, "that's what his pal keeps telling him."

Finally, Veronica mentioned the pressure they were under from Len's brother.

Following his intimidating letters, Walter had now started phoning, threatening to come round and seize his brother's ashes. Veronica hadn't let Walter talk directly to Andrew but, as she told Jenny, her brother was aware that something was going on, and it was stress he could well do without.

Later that same day, Veronica found Andrew in the spare room, pouring over some old photograph albums that she'd unearthed.

"We're not throwing this out," Andrew said. "It's got me and Len in it, youth hostelling." He held up the album for her to see.

"My goodness, aren't you both young!" She looked more closely. "Isn't that Falling Foss?" she said, pointing to one tiny snap.

"Aye, it is," said Andrew, his Yorkshire accent suddenly more pronounced. "One of us favourite spots," he added.

"You know, he took *me* there once," Veronica said, colouring slightly.

"Len did?" Andrew looked shocked. "He never said!"

"Well, perhaps he didn't share everything with you!" she asserted. "I, too, was young once, *tha' knows*!" She too could lay on the accent. They sat awhile, lost in their memories. Then Veronica said, "You know what, Andrew? Falling Foss would be an excellent spot for Len's ashes."

"Now, that's a grand idea."

"In fact," added Veronica, looking at Walter's letters gathered on the mantelpiece, "we should get ourselves there as soon as possible."

Andrew's eyes lit up.

Andrew was so enthusiastic, despite his fragile state, that Veronica agreed they should make the journey first thing in the morning. She'd pick up a wheelchair *en route* and, if Andrew was up to it, they'd round off the day with a fish supper in Whitby.

❁

The following day, when they were about halfway there, Veronica turned to her brother and asked, "What was that phrase Len kept saying to you?"

"Falling fast," said Andrew.

"Falling fast … Falling Foss," mused Veronica.

Andrew looked quizzically at her before the penny dropped. Then he started laughing, although the pain in his stomach quickly arrested him.

"Don't you dare burst those stitches," said Veronica.

"No," answered Andrew. "But it's all alright now … because I'm not … falling fast!"

"You never were, you daft ha'porth!"

"If I hadn't been so deaf," began Andrew, "I might have heard him properly … or if Len hadn't such a broad accent …"

"Listen, brother of mine. Len never was speaking to you, so you never could have misheard him. It was all in your noggin. You were just deaf to what your subconscious kept trying to tell you."

Andrew tried to turn in his seat and address the casket seat-belted in the back. "You hear that, old friend?"

Veronica pretended to ignore him, focusing on the road ahead. But she couldn't keep a straight face for long, and the two ended up giggling like kids.

Although Andrew's abdomen throbbed with pain, he didn't mind in the slightest. Indeed, he was revelling in how alive that ache made him feel.

He turned to his sister and declared, quite loudly, "Falling fast. Nay, lass. Rising steadily!"

Doomsday Davidson

"CONTROVERSIAL   PAINTER
VANISHES"
"DOOMSDAY FOR DAVIDSON"
"DERANGED DAVIDSON DISAPPEARS"

It's now almost twenty years since those headlines, following Charles Davidson's strange disappearance in 1965. As someone who knew him well, it was to my door that the media initially came. At the time, I told them nothing, but as I now start to feel my years, I realise I ought to set down these biographical observations.

I had known Davidson since we were both at a minor public school in the 1930s. I was his oldest friend, there's no doubt about that. Back in those early days, I can't say we were very close, but I would certainly count myself one of his confidants.

Davidson (I always called him by his surname – a hangover from public school, I suppose) was drawing those eerie cityscapes even as a fifteen-year-old. Indeed, I don't think his style changed at all, though I have read critics who try to chart its subtle development. As far as I'm concerned, his pictures were always and forever the same: paintings that seemed to envelop you in their gloomy depths. His modern-day evocations of Piranesi-style buildings made you feel infinitesimal, incapable of comprehending their vastness, and you began to think that these constructions were never intended for mortal eyes. You can imagine their initial impact on me, as a teenager, especially knowing that one of my contemporaries was creating such visionary stuff.

I think one of the best descriptions of his work came from a critic intending to be dismissive, who said that Davidson's work gave viewers an unsolicited, first-hand experience of modern-building syndrome. However misguided that critic's intentions, he hit the nail on the head, for Davidson's canvases are undoubtedly disorienting. One minute you are standing there, an outsider, gazing at one of his decaying cityscapes; the next, you find yourself trapped within, seeking a way to escape their oppressive depths.

For those that knew the man, his paintings seemed even more incongruous, for they were on such a grand scale, whereas Davidson himself was a small, dapper chap, always wearing those round, wire spectacles that seemed to distance him from his surroundings. He looked more like a banker than a painter. In fact, Magritte's bowler-hatted figure comes to mind – especially apposite when one recalls the surreal world that Magritte's anonymous men inhabited.

After we left school – Davidson going off to the Slade, me to the University of Exeter – we lost touch for a number of years. When I next encountered him, in the late 1940s, he was in his twenties and already an established artist. I came across him in a small pub in Soho. It had been a fruitful morning on my part, touring the antiquarian bookshops around Charing Cross, buying some military history on behalf of a collector. It was Davidson who grabbed me – and grabbed is the word. He tugged at my sleeve, as though I were some crook he was apprehending. The man was certainly the worse for drink.

"I can't keep going," he declared.

I wondered whether he had really recognised me or, in the manner of some Ancient Mariner, was just buttonholing anyone who would listen to him. It was not the sort of greeting one expected from a long-lost school-friend.

"It's Davidson, isn't it?" I said.

He physically recoiled.

"Day vision," he said. At first I thought he was struggling with his wayward tongue, but then he added, "More like night vision!" And I realised that, in his sardonic way, he was being serious. "Doomsday Davidson – child prodigy," he continued. "Treading in the muddy footsteps of Fuseli, Piranesi and Blake-y … and some would rather he didn't …" His voice trailed off, as though he were walking out of earshot.

"Do you not know me, old man?" I demanded, sounding like someone out of *King Lear*.

He looked at me more intently through those globular specs, then seemed to break out of whatever mental turmoil possessed him. "Course I do. It's …," he surprised himself, "Worthington. Colin Worthington!" There was a pause before he added, "That's why I came across." His eyes twinkled mischievously.

"Well, it's good to see you, old man," I said. "Do you drink here regularly?"

"If you mean, do I do a lot of drinking here, I suppose the answer's yes. It's the watering hole closest to my studio."

We then began reminiscing about the good old days and must have talked for an hour or so before he invited me back to his studio. As I seemed to be having such a positive effect on him, I readily agreed.

The studio was a revelation – and a nightmare. It was crammed with those intimidating canvases of his, which, *en masse* and up close, are even more disquieting. They envelop you, each canvas like a building block from one of his monstrous cityscapes. I am not claustrophobic by nature but, as I said before, his paintings give you a horribly oppressive feeling: the great girders of those buildings bearing down, casting malevolent shadows; those pulleys descending from giant beams, disporting ropes from which noose-like shapes tantalisingly dangle.

And these were just the easy, familiar parts of his paintings, those that you could put a name to. Beyond them, indescribable clots of shadow sucked at your eyeballs. You really didn't want to look too closely, but you couldn't help yourself. It was as though you'd been strapped to a rack and someone had peeled back your eyelids, forcing you to gawp. Trapped, you found yourself clinging tenaciously to those more tangible elements: the huge metal beams, the ropes and chains.

I still find his canvases hard to describe – as you can tell – and I've yet to find a critic who doesn't fall prey to some comforting cliché in order to tame Davidson's visions.

Davidson was clearly attentive to my initial reaction in that studio. "Not pretty, are they?" he joked, as we navigated the cluttered rooms.

We hadn't been in there more than ten minutes before Davidson grabbed me by the arm again, as he had done in the pub.

"Come on," he demanded, and hustled me back into the airy street. "Sorry to put you through that. Just needed to see your reaction."

"I don't think I could live with those paintings of yours," I confessed. "At school, they seemed quite appealing, but …" I was lost for words.

"Let's get some coffee," he said.

Looking back, I must have encountered him at exactly the right moment. He opened up as though he'd been ready to burst, and I am glad that I, who had known him so long, was there to respond. After our conversation, I felt far closer to Davidson.

It was at this initial reunion that he told me he had several more studios, just like the one we'd visited, all chock-full of his canvases.

"Are they not selling, then?" I ventured.

He laughed. "They *sell* – my agent certainly shifts a fair few – but they also have a tendency to come back! 'Boomerang art', he calls it. Some people simply consign the things to the attic. You'd be surprised how many houses have a Davidson tucked away somewhere." He chuckled. "When art collectors of the future start going through people's lofts, they'll find more than they bargained for," he broke off with another strained laugh. "Of course, many punters simply get rid of the things. Burned mostly."

"People burn your canvases? Surely …"

"No, no," he interrupted, before conceding the point. "Well, for all I know they might! But I was thinking of the ones that I, personally, dispose of for their owners. I must have saved the world hundreds of Davidsons already."

"But … why? I mean, why paint them in the first place?"

"*I* paint them?" He looked at me, strangely. "*They* paint *me*, more like."

Davidson later became renowned for this sort of claim. And certainly, if you'd ever seen him at his easel – I believe there is some footage of him at work – you'd know that his style is quite manic, often working with his eyes shut, as though in thrall to some inner vision. However, on this occasion, I tried to make light of his comment. "The driven artist, eh?"

"Don't, old chap. I know you mean well, but I'm not like those posers you see in studios nowadays, fuelled on alcohol, attacking canvases as though possessed." He paused, then burst out laughing. "Actually, I'm exactly like them, aren't I? Or appear to be. I wonder if there *are* others … equally tormented?"

Our conversation then drifted from what was obviously a distressing topic. But we agreed to meet again. Indeed, he demanded it, making me promise before he would let go of my arm.

After that, we met up almost every week. I would like to say that he became more at ease as a result. But maybe I presume too much. Whatever was the case, I certainly got to know more about Davidson, the "tortured" artist (and I use that overworked epithet with care).

He told me that, since puberty, he had produced at least five canvases a day – and sometimes a great many more. He also told me that he couldn't stop this rate of production. Not because he was inspired so much as because he felt compelled, fearing the consequences of not painting.

At some point, he produced an old scrapbook which I at first thought must contain reviews of his exhibitions. It did not. It was full of illustrations of now familiar atrocities: images of skeletal bodies and mutilated corpses; the death camps, Hiroshima, the Burmese railway. I must say, we nearly fell out over his scrapbook. I got the wrong end of the stick entirely, thinking that this sort of stuff inspired him. I mean, I know that some artists, like Goya and Francis Bacon, found inspiration in this direction.

"Ins*pired*," he spat out. "It doesn't *inspire* me! I paint to prevent this sort of thing happening."

I must have looked completely blank, for his spectacled eyes were suddenly fiery, boring into my own.

"When I try to stop, as I did in the early 1950s," his voice became slow and measured, "something unspeakable happens like … like the atrocities of the Algerian War." He broke off for a while. "It's quite simple, really. The more I paint, the safer the world is."

"Come on, old man," I said. I don't know why we called each other old man – probably another hangover from public school days – but in his case it seemed most apposite. Although still relatively young, he spoke as though he had been around for aeons, like some hapless Wandering Jew. "Come on," I repeated, trying to make light of his claim about saving the world through painting. I'm not a psychologically oriented person, but I was sure there was a name for the sort of condition he presented: paranoia, schizophrenia, that sort of thing. "It's just a coincidence."

He'd obviously had this conversation many times before. "I know what you're thinking. I've wished it were so myself, but the evidence is against it." Again, those gimlet eyes were on me. "When I first began painting seriously, that's when all those bloody conflicts," he gestured to his scrapbook, "came to an end."

"Even so … I mean … it can't just be you…" I was annoyed with myself for even giving him the benefit of the doubt. "It just can't be," I ended feebly.

I have reported the above as though it were one conversation, but it's an amalgam of many similar discussions we had. Conversations that Davidson would usually initiate, only to shut them down, exasperatingly, shortly thereafter.

Another event in his life that had obviously had a huge impact was his relationship with Judy Bigma, whom he'd met at the Slade. He was more expansive about her. She had been his first serious girlfriend. Apparently, she'd tried to restrict his painting so that they might spend more time together. She used to hide his paints and brushes. With her, it seemed to have worked; he had complied. They were clearly very much in love. Indeed, he told me as much.

But then she fell ill: a period of delirium with a high temperature, quickly leading to a catatonic state that mystified everyone. As Davidson tells it, he spent many hours by her bedside, initially respecting her wish that he shouldn't paint. But then the craving became too strong, and – well, I happen to have his account recorded on my old tape recorder, so I'll let him tell it:

> I seized her lipstick and started
> scrawling over the paper that her
> flowers were wrapped in. The usual
> shapes started to appear under my
> hand, albeit smudged and messy,
> until there was a whole lattice
> of beams on the paper – great
> fortifications that seemed capable
> of containing the negative energy
> emanating from her.
>
> When I'd finished, I looked
> up to see Judy staring at me.
> She hadn't stirred for weeks, yet
> here she was: back, conscious! I
> summoned the nurse, and the story
> of her remarkable recovery soon
> went round the hospital. I *knew*
> the two events were connected: *my*
> drawing and *her* recovery. More
> importantly, I knew that my initial
> failure to act had been the cause

of her deterioration. I couldn't tell anyone else, of course. They'd have thought me mad.

Our relationship never really recovered, though. Judy had been incensed seeing me at her bedside, doing the very thing she'd asked me not to. She could never understand that that is what had saved her.

Unfortunately, my machine has chewed up the rest of the tape. But Davidson said little more of interest. He became increasingly morose and clammed up. Undoubtedly, though, Judy's illness had a huge impact on him. That was when he really started painting like a man on a mission.

"Painting," as he always liked to say, "keeps the monsters at bay."

I am aware that this memoir is sounding increasingly implausible but, as I said earlier, I need to set it down for the record – for my own sake if for no other. So please bear with me.

To fully understand Davidson's outlook, you need to know a bit more than I've already told you, for he held to the strange belief that this world we inhabit has a dark underside. Manichaeism, is it? Don't ask me how it all works but, in simple terms, Davidson would refer to another realm, deep beneath the surface of the earth. He would always point downwards when speaking of it, though he also seemed to see it as being inside us. This other world was – *is*, in his terms – a strange, oppressive place, consisting of huge caverns in which dark, shadowy, half-formed creatures exist. And, as you've already seen, it's the world of his pictures.

Davidson believed that this underground realm was always in danger of erupting, of invading our own world and, as a result, causing violence and destruction. In some of his notebooks – which have yet to see the light of day – he has tried to explain much of this, pointing to various episodes in history when irrational behaviour has been at its most virulent and destructive.

So, Davidson saw himself in that very ancient, but now unfashionable role of an artist who suffers on behalf of mankind. As far as he was concerned, those canvases with their intimidating grids and lattices were his attempt to contain that destructive internal world, to keep the enemy in check. In fact, he often said that he was like a locksmith, except that, instead of oiling cogs, he oiled canvases.

I didn't really take Davidson too seriously when he started expounding this stuff, although I always tried to be a receptive audience. But then he performed that disappearing trick. He was always unpredictable, so I wasn't too surprised at first. Perhaps some sort of bender or reclusive retreat? It could have been any number of things.

But after a few weeks – just before the police launched a missing persons investigation, in fact – I paid a visit to his Soho studio. I hadn't been there for quite a while, but I did know where he hid his keys. By Davidson's claustrophobic standards, the flat was not quite full, but I immediately felt that old revulsion as the canvases seemed to close in on me. I might have been alright but for the heavy reek of oil and turps, which turned me quite nauseous and, after only a few minutes, I headed back towards the front door, unable to breathe. In the hallway – one of the few areas with any floorspace – I stumbled into his easel, on which was mounted what was, presumably, his final canvas.

In my haste, I dislodged the painting and it came crashing down on me. Instinctively, as though it were attacking me, I fended it off. As I propped it back on the easel, I looked at it more carefully than I would otherwise have done. Massive pillars stood in the foreground but, behind one, and seemingly out of place, lurked a figure. Without a doubt, I could discern a hand, a hand reaching out towards me and, behind it, an anguished face. Not just any face. It was Davidson's, I swear! Having realised this, I looked more attentively. Wasn't there a paintbrush in his hand – that hand on the wrong side of the canvas – seeking, so it seemed to me, to give more painterly weight to the oppressive fortifications that contained him?

I saw no more. I fled, only returning under escort when the police investigation was underway. That final painting was still on the easel, but I looked in vain for his trapped figure. All I could see was a smudgy cocoon of paint where I thought Davidson had once been. I still have nightmares about this diminutive version of the man, arm outstretched on the wrong side of the canvas. In these dreams, Davidson invariably becomes enveloped in sticky black threads exuding from large spidery creatures (and I've since discerned similar arachnid forms in other canvases of his).

I know. You must think that I too am of "unsound mind". And that's something I also worry about. But Davidson's fate remains a mystery. His body has never been found. And, of course, this whole intrigue had a huge impact on his estate. The value of his paintings soared. At auction, even semi-charred canvases of his command record figures.

Personally, I've kept a low profile (this memoir being the one exception), although nowadays I do keep a closer eye on world conflicts. Is it just me, or are they really spreading? Davidson's disappearance had barely been acknowledged before the Indo-Pakistani War broke out, featuring the worst military hardware battles since World War II. The Vietnam War was also escalating, there were "the Troubles" in Northern Ireland, the Six-Day War, the Nigerian Civil War – well, the list is endless. And I can't help but contrast this with the period when Davidson started painting professionally, shortly after he and Judy Bigma separated in the late 1940s. Peace in our time, they were declaring, and then came the Welfare State and the Marshall Plan.

I'm not one for moral panic and media hype, but I do find myself looking round at Davidson's canvases in a more sympathetic way nowadays. I have several mounted around our home, despite my wife's protests.

I'd like to think that out there, somewhere, there might be a younger artist, someone with Davidson's peculiar gift, who is even now honing their skills, trying to construct an effective barrier against what lies without – or, more accurately, within. Perhaps an entire school of artists could be tasked with such a project. Would the MOD fund it?

But then I can also imagine the hysterical reaction that would greet any mention of his name, given the public's memory of "Deranged Doomsday Davidson!" They'd have a field day, and they'd probably lock me up too, although I'm not sure that being behind bars would make me feel any more secure.

Perhaps, if we could just persuade more galleries to display his works, to fund international touring exhibitions.

Perhaps … perhaps that might help.

On the Threshold

Wallace woke in the early hours, as he so frequently did. This time it wasn't for the toilet. He'd got up earlier for that … hadn't he? Or was that the night before? This time, it was a noise from downstairs that had disturbed him. It sounded like someone breaking in.

Nowadays, Wallace was fearful of burglars. He couldn't get over how frail he'd become. In the past he'd have tackled anyone. Had them out on their ear. Now he was just a "poor old codger". He'd heard people say it: needed a stick to walk; was blind as a bat without his specs; and deaf to boot. And that was aside from his "prostrate" problems, as he termed them.

Wallace looked round for his clock but, without his specs, couldn't read the time anyway. It was certainly still night-time. The sounds downstairs continued. Someone was definitely entering his property, but it was not a break-in; that was the front door he'd heard closing. Had he forgotten to lock it? The other night, he'd even left the gas on, unlit. What was he coming to?

Now there were voices in the hall. Two of them, was it? This was serious. Downstairs, a light clicked on.

"I wouldn't have troubled you, but you did say, if we heard anything."

"I'm much obliged to you, Colin."

The second voice sounded like his son, Robert. Wallace wanted to call out to him but couldn't get his mouth to work. Besides which, his teeth were in the bathroom.

Robert, Wallace now realised, was talking to Colin Brown, Wallace's neighbour. Always checking up on him, were Colin and Sally. Nice enough couple but far too nosy.

"When I heard a few bangs and thumps, I thought I should let you know," continued Colin. "It sounded ominous."

The voices grew louder as they reached the staircase. Wallace's stairs ran up the middle of the terraced house, his being one of the few properties that hadn't been modernised.

"Oh, Jesus!" Wallace heard his son exclaim. Unusual to hear him swear.

"You'd best ring Emergency Services," said Colin. "Is there a pulse?"

Who on earth were they talking about? wondered Wallace. Was there someone on his stairs? Was it the burglar he thought he'd heard earlier? He wanted to shout out but still couldn't get his mouth working. He cursed silently.

He must have fallen asleep again, for he was suddenly conscious of more noise. A vehicle in the street, doors opening and closing, more people coming into his front room.

"And you are Mr Robert Godfrey," enquired a female voice, "son of Wallace Godfrey?"

"He's on the stairs," said Robert. "Just a faint pulse. We tried not to move him."

"No!" Wallace wanted to shout, but his jaw was slack. They'd got the wrong person. He needed to tell them. He tried to raise himself, but his muscles wouldn't respond. Whoever was on the stairs, it wasn't him. And why hadn't Robert come up to see him, to warn him about this strange body on his stairs? He could have fallen over it.

Just then, Wallace experienced a peculiar sensation. He wasn't in his bedroom anymore. He was gazing down at some uniformed people on the stairs, huddled round a body. He could hear Robert and Colin in the background. Then he noticed that it was his body they were crouched round.

It gave him a jolt that triggered a memory of getting up earlier in the night. He'd been heading for the loo – one of his regular visits – when he'd felt some stabbing pains in his feet which made him lose his balance. He looked down at the small, crumpled figure lying there, like a … like a poor old codger!

But, if that was him, who was he, watching all this? And who was in his bed? With this thought, he suddenly found himself gazing down at his empty bed. It was very disorienting. Was he dreaming all this?

No, he thought, that's not it. He felt untethered, like a helium balloon after its owner has let go the string. He found he could go anywhere, just by thinking of it, as he discovered when he heard a noise outside. Immediately he was at his bedroom window, gazing down at the street below, where he could see one of the ambulance crew fetching something.

Am I dying, then? was Wallace's next thought, which, although not spoken, sounded quite brashly in his head.

The instant after he'd expressed it, another presence in his head responded with, "Good question. I wondered when you'd think of that."

"Who are you?" demanded Wallace. His house was like Piccadilly Circus tonight.

"Don't you recognise your old Dad?"

"You! Are you … in my head?"

"I'm all around, son. Just like yourself. As you'll find out."

"Are there others here, too?"

"Others?"

"Mum?"

"Nah. She died in the mental hospital, didn't she?"

Wallace had hardly framed his questions before his father's replies were inside his head.

His father went on. "That's the thing, see. You need to die here for your spirit to survive. Otherwise, you're gone, for good."

"Does that mean … it's just you and me?"

"When you go, it is!"

"I'm not dead yet?"

"Nah. On your way, though. That's why you've begun to separate from your body there."

Immediately his father said this, Wallace found himself once again looking down the stairs.

"That's also why we can communicate. But it's crucial you die before you leave this house."

As Wallace floated around on his landing, something unusual caught his eye and he asked his father, "Can you do stuff as a spirit? You know, move objects and that?"

"You can create all kinds of mischief if you've a mind. Polterghosts, that's us. Bert and Wallace – we're a team!"

"So, spreading tacks at the top of the stairs. That'd be you, would it?"

"Now, son. What you saying?"

"That you're a selfish old git, Bert Godfrey," declared Wallace, "and always were – which is why Mum left."

"Mum lost her marbles."

"You smashed all her marbles."

"Now don't start on all that again."

"You planned this, didn't you?

"Son, your time's up."

"But you thought you'd hurry things along."

Their talk was halted by raised voices.

"Thought he was a goner, but now he's rallied," said Suzy, the female paramedic. "Better get him to A&E."

Wallace could feel the exasperation steaming off his father, followed by a sense that he was no longer inside his head. He listened more carefully to the conversation below.

"I need a drink," he heard Robert say. "Anyone else for a cuppa?"

"If you're quick," said Suzy. "We'll get your dad ready for the ambulance."

Robert went to the kitchen, but no sooner had he entered than Wallace heard him swearing again. Most uncharacteristic. He heard the back door and kitchen windows being flung open. Robert returned to the ambulance crew. "God, the rotten egg smell in Dad's kitchen. Only left the gas on, hadn't he? I daren't light the stove now. And he's got no electric kettle."

"Old folks are forgetful," said Dan, Suzy's colleague.

"I'll nip home and make us a brew," said Colin.

Wallace strained to project his thoughts. "Where are you, Dad? It was you, wasn't it, turned on the gas?" Wallace envisaged himself shouting out these words.

"What you on about, son?" came the instant reply.

"And last night," continued Wallace, the insight suddenly striking him. "There was me, thinking I was getting forgetful with the gas, and it was you all the time." In his head, Wallace saw himself yelling this at full pitch. "You try to blow me up, topple me to my death – anything to make sure I don't leave here alive."

"Blow you up?" Bert sounded genuinely offended. "Never crossed my mind."

Wallace realised his dad might have a point. "Of course, it was coal gas in your day, wasn't it, full of carbon monoxide? You were trying to poison me then, weren't you?" There was no reply. Wallace's thoughts ran on. "Won't work with natural gas, though. Only blow us up. One naked flame and whomp!"

"As if," snorted Bert. "But listen son. As I keep telling you, if they take you out that front door before you've popped your clogs, we're lost."

"Selfish to the end."

"I'm thinking of you, son," the voice wheedled. "We could share old times together."

"Over my dead body," said Wallace, chuckling at the irony.

Bert, though, had taken himself off to the kitchen where, inspired by Wallace and Robert, he once again secured the windows and back door before turning on every gas tap he could find: the hob burners, the grill, the oven and, finally, the tap for the water heater.

Meanwhile, Dan had nipped out the front, supposedly to fetch something from the ambulance. Really, he was desperate for a smoke. He only managed a few drags before he heard Suzy yelling. Turning back towards the house, he got the shock of his life.

The sound – more of a wail – had not come from Suzy but from a decapitated head protruding through the front door. It was like Marley's ghost, with wiry hair and bulging eyeballs, and it was staring at Dan, who immediately dropped his cigarette and locked himself in the ambulance.

Chuckling, the rest of Bert's form eased itself through the door. He picked up the cigarette and went down the back passage to Wallace's yard. There, he opened the back door and let the ciggie do the rest.

"Whoomp," said the kitchen.

Bert chuckled to himself.

Inside, Suzy had given up waiting for Dan. She and Robert had begun stretchering Wallace, while Colin opened the front door. The blast accelerated their departure.

Colin took himself straight home, anxious for his family and property. He soon returned and, with a few other neighbours, tried to douse the flames emanating from Wallace's property.

Robert and Suzy discovered a sheepish Dan cowering in the back of the ambulance. Suzy shouted for him to call the police and fire brigade while she hooked Wallace up to the monitors. Robert sat with his dad.

Dan went through to the cab, still in shock. Wallace was the only one who appeared relaxed, a vague smile playing across his dry lips.

"It's funny," said Robert, "Dad always said he'd end his days here, where he was born. Said they'd have to drag him out feet first."

"Well, he's not done yet," said Suzy, patting Robert's shoulder. "And he came out head first – not feet – which is probably how he was born."

Their smiles were arrested by a horrible wailing sound, which many in the street mistook for a police siren. Dan immediately started the engine, shouting through for everyone to strap up.

"Are you alright, partner?" asked Suzy, joining Dan in the cab. "You look like you've seen a ghost."

Dan accelerated away without comment.

They both heard the bleep of Wallace's heart monitor stutter to a halt.

Robert also heard it. He turned to his dad, who, he was pleased to see, looked at peace. As he said to Suzy and Dan, his father appeared happier than he'd done for a while. As Robert stared at his dad's wrinkled old face, he could have sworn that that ridiculous, toothless smile of his was spreading wider than ever.

Fear of Flying Freehold

"What's flying freehold?" asked Jenny – Susan and Richard's eight-year-old daughter – as they sat in the kitchen amidst the chaos of their move. Boxes and crates were piled around them, abandoned by the removal men.

"Flying freehold is that bit of our house that sits on top of next door's lounge," explained Susan, "as if it was flying."

"Don't they mind us being up there?" asked Jenny.

"Not legally," laughed Richard, though they'd all been aware that Mrs Duxbury, one half of the elderly couple from next door, had been wandering round the front garden, looking at them suspiciously, and occasionally getting under the removal team's feet as she wandered into their lorry.

Susan and Richard's flying freehold had an interesting history. Until fairly recently, it seemed that the owners of the two, semi-detached Victorian properties had swapped the "flying" bit on several occasions, depending on who had the greater need at the time – usually because of growing families. In those days, it was done amicably. Lawyers weren't involved. However, the families in question had also been related.

Now, it was very different. In fact, Susan and Richard's solicitor had cautioned them against purchasing the property. Certainly, obtaining a mortgage had been next to impossible, but when Susan's mother had suddenly died, bequeathing them the necessary capital, they'd gone ahead. They'd fallen in love with this old house, Jenny especially.

The only stumbling block had been the TA6. This was the form the vendor was required to complete, providing information about the state of the property, with comments about the neighbours and neighbourhood. It transpired that the Oldhams, the previous owners, had made some negative comments about the Duxburys. The former had been denied access to the Duxbury's land when they had wanted to renovate the window frame in the flying freehold.

Although it sounded problematic – which was why their solicitor had advised them to drop it – Susan had talked personally to Mr Duxbury, a man in his eighties. He was very accommodating, apologising for their seeming obstructiveness. His wife, he explained, had dementia and suffered with her nerves, so he'd asked the Oldhams to delay their repairs until his wife's respite care. "Unfortunately," as Mr Duxbury had told Susan, "they went ahead straightaway. Mr Oldham erected some homemade scaffolding on his side of the fence and, well, you know the rest. Most regrettable."

Susan certainly did know about Mr Oldham's Heath Robinson scaffolding, which had stretched across from his side of the fence to the Duxbury's, only to collapse soon after he'd mounted it, resulting in an emergency visit to A&E.

After this mishap, the Oldhams had put their house up for sale. It had certainly hung about on the market – mainly because of that flying freehold – with the Oldhams dropping their price several times. This was how it had come within Susan and Richard's grasp.

Jenny had been very excited at the prospect of occupying the flying freehold room. It was certainly quirky, with capacious built-in cupboards and a large mahogany wardrobe across the end wall, which abutted the Duxbury's property. The moment she'd seen it, Jenny had fallen in love with the room.

In fact, she savoured every nook and cranny of the house and garden. She wanted to live there forever, she'd informed her parents. But her favourite room remained her flying freehold, which she arranged to her liking. Each of her toys, including her extensive collection of furry animals, was allocated its distinct place.

Jenny also announced that she'd discovered a special friend called Wendy, who played with her in her room. Her parents weren't happy about this, but Jenny's teacher assured them that imaginary friends were a common phenomenon, often lasting until puberty. When they asked, "Why now?", the teacher put it down to the disruption of the move.

Things were fine for several months until, one morning, Susan found herself unintentionally yelling as she'd gone in to wake Jenny. Beneath her instep Susan discovered an unyielding lump. After stumbling over several more pieces, Susan reached the curtains and cast some light on things. They both stared at the floor, Lego and soft toys scattered all over.

"What you done, Mummy?" said Jenny, roused by her mother's cries.

"Me!" exclaimed Susan. "I was going to ask *you* that."

"It must have been Wendy."

"Wendy! Of course! She's made a bit of a mess, hasn't she?"

"Sorry, Mummy. She is a bit untidy." Jenny leapt out of bed. "I can clear it up."

They both set to. Susan was keen not to make an issue of it – in line with the teacher's advice – but she was worried about Jenny being up in the night, playing. Had Jenny, her mum wondered, actually been awake, or had she been sleepwalking, or sleep-playing?

This sort of disruption began to occur more regularly. "Doesn't Wendy like to sleep at nights?" Susan had asked her daughter.

"Yes, but she also likes playing in the dark. We're going to have a midnight feast, next."

"Really? And will you be ordering in food for that?"

Susan shared her concerns with Richard, who thought it was nothing to worry about. "Wendy's an *imaginary* friend. What could go wrong?"

Nevertheless, even though imaginary, both Susan and Richard found themselves checking on Jenny whenever either woke in the night. Not that they ever saw anything untoward, but Susan was concerned about some of the activities Jenny mentioned. She was particularly disturbed when Jenny said that Wendy had shown her how to fly round the room, "without holding on, cos that's why it's called flying freehold." Even though Susan had recently read *Peter Pan* to her daughter – which is where she supposed Jenny had come up with the name Wendy – Susan was still concerned at the thought of Jenny clambering onto her chest of drawers at night.

And, speaking of *Peter Pan*, Susan was upset to discover, one morning, her childhood copy of that book, along with others, scattered across Jenny's floor, some with their pages torn.

Susan was not sure what to say to Jenny. Was her daughter learning the art of deception? Was Wendy nothing but a scapegoat? Jenny had already admitted that her friend wasn't a physical presence; more like something that existed in her head.

However, the games that Jenny played seemed a bit old fashioned. She'd once found Jenny's crayons laid out in a grid on the floor. "For hopscotch," Jenny had said. Another time, Susan had found her doing some fancy skipping with her dressing-gown cord. "Where did you learn that?" Susan had asked, only to be told that Wendy had shown her.

It was after the incident with the books that Susan had run into Valerie Oldham in town. They'd first met when Susan and Richard went to view the house, which is when they'd heard about Mr Oldham's accident. The two women now went for a coffee.

When Valerie asked how they were settling in, Susan mentioned Jenny's nocturnal behaviour. Valerie admitted that their son, Max, who was a couple of years older than Jenny, had never liked the room, refusing, in the end, to sleep in it.

"We had to move him. It was strange because it was only then that Mrs Duxbury started causing trouble. You must have seen her wandering about, bent over like some fairy-tale witch?" Susan smiled as Valerie did her witch impression. "We'd get scribbled notes poked through our letterbox at all hours, complaining about the noise and disturbance. Mr D was very apologetic about his wife, saying it was the dementia. But, even so, there can't have been any noise after Max had left that room. It was only used for storage" – she paused for a moment before leaning over confidentially – "though we did occasionally find our boxes overturned, their contents spilled out. That's when we started blaming the poltergeist, but I think it must have been Max being mischievous."

The word poltergeist shook Susan. It was not something she'd previously contemplated. It was not something, after all, one would ever see declared on a TA6 form.

That evening, Susan once again voiced her concerns about Wendy to Richard. They found themselves in a quandary for, unlike Max, Jenny loved her room and wouldn't abandon it for anything.

In the end, Susan decided she'd spend the next few nights sleeping with their daughter. Richard was going away on a three-day course, so it was a reasonable arrangement. It would certainly give Susan a chance to observe Jenny's nocturnal habits close-up.

❧ 🌟 ☙

Her first night with Jenny was exhausting. It was windy and the damaged window frame rattled, which certainly didn't help Susan's nerves. Every time Jenny stirred,

Susan found herself wide awake, her head bursting with irrational thoughts. At one point, she imagined some malevolent presence flying above them, circling their bed. Susan envisaged her own head tracking it, rotating like the possessed girl in *The Exorcist*.

She must finally have dropped off, but woke with a jolt as she felt the bed shudder. Once again, *The Exorcist* came to mind, but it was only Jenny, standing by the bed, shaking her.

"Wake up, Mummy, it's breakfast time."

Susan surfaced from what felt like a night on the tiles. Then she saw, once again, books and heaps of Lego scattered over the floor. She shot out of bed, grabbing Jenny by the shoulders. "What happened?"

"Nothing, Mummy. I was just playing polty-ghosts, waiting for you to wake up."

Jenny's remark was innocent, but it distressed Susan. "Poltergeist," she corrected her daughter, before realising it was not a concept she wanted to encourage.

The following evening, even more exhausted, Susan again bedded down with Jenny. She fell asleep almost immediately and was soon dreaming wildly about the two of them, airborne, circling the room. Wendy was showing them how to perform aerial somersaults. Susan woke in a sweat before realising she'd been re-enacting *Peter Pan*. Flying freehold, indeed!

By the third night, Susan had lost the will to live. She couldn't wait for Richard's return.

Jenny found it highly amusing that her mother was falling asleep over their bedtime story. "Perhaps *I* should read to *you*," she chuckled.

Susan mumbled something incoherent before starting to snore, leaving Jenny to switch off the bedside light.

Susan slept well until dawn. Then she experienced what seemed another nightmare. Lying with her head towards the mahogany wardrobe, she watched as its big doors swung open, revealing the clothes hanging inside. She then saw one of the outfits detach itself from its hanger and step out of the wardrobe. Susan gazed at this vision, transfixed. It was as though she were trapped in another childhood classic: *The Lion, the Witch and the Wardrobe*.

Eventually, it dawned on her that she was not dreaming. She was awake and the figure she observed moving with slow deliberation was no fairy-tale witch. It was Mrs Duxbury. At this realisation, Susan was jolted into full consciousness and shot bolt upright.

Despite the darkness, her sudden movement must have caught Mrs Duxbury's eye, for the bent figure gave a small gasp before turning on her heel and fighting her way back into the depths of the wardrobe. Susan looked down at Jenny, who slept on, oblivious.

Susan experienced a mix of emotions. She was incensed at Mrs Duxbury's bizarre invasion, but relieved that it was only their neighbour – a living being, not a ghost – even though she might yet prove to be something witchy.

Jenny's regular breathing gradually calmed Susan. She slid out of her daughter's bed and approached the wardrobe. She stepped inside and explored the rear of the carcass, but could find nothing untoward. A full investigation would have to wait until morning.

The next thing she knew, it was 7.30 a.m. Once again, Jenny was tugging on her arm, insistently intoning, "Mummy, wake up."

Ignoring the wardrobe, Susan and Jenny dressed and got on with their day.

Back home after driving Jenny to school, and with the next few hours to herself, Susan returned to the wardrobe, threw its doors wide open and pushed the clothes aside to probe the back panelling. It was dark within, but Susan had come prepared with her phone torch. "Narnia, here we come," she muttered to herself.

Ever since she'd first seen this magnificent wardrobe, it had been on her mind to read that children's classic to Jenny. Then it had seemed an apposite choice, but now she was nervous of sharing it. Did she really want Jenny – along with Wendy, too, no doubt – probing in here? However, despite pushing and prodding with her fingernails, Susan could find no moving parts. She gave up.

As she went back downstairs, another thought jolted her. Could Mrs Duxbury and Wendy be one and the same? Was it Mrs D that Jenny was playing with in the night? Surely not. Jenny would have said something.

Determined to get to the bottom of things, Susan decided it was time to pay their neighbours a visit. She had intended to wait until Richard returned, but she was too impatient. That woman had some explaining to do, dementia or not.

The wind was taken out of her sails when Mr Duxbury answered the door. Had his wife, who was always wandering around, gone to ground, perhaps? Too embarrassed to answer the door?

He was a tall man with a slight stoop, emphasised by his cardigan which, thanks to bulging pockets at the front, hung distended. On his feet were a pair of threadbare slippers. He led her into their kitchen and offered her coffee, which she declined.

They spent a while exchanging pleasantries. He asked how they were settling in, although they'd already been there several months. He also surprised her by saying how delightful it was to have a youngster back in the house, "next door, I mean," he clarified.

Susan found his friendly manner disconcerting, given the concerns she wanted to raise. And where was Mrs D?

When he asked whether Jenny had made any new friends, Susan seized the moment.

"She's made an imaginary friend," Susan replied, "called Wendy."

Mr Duxbury's face sagged visibly. Susan knew she'd hit a nerve but pressed on, "And last night we had a visitor in our flying freehold."

His face slumped further. "You'd better come upstairs," he said, leading the way. "Elsie's asleep at the moment …" But he was brought up short as, negotiating the turn in the stairs, Mrs Duxbury was there, in her nightdress, standing at the top.

"Hello dear," he said.

She didn't reply.

As they reached the first floor, he took his wife's arm and steered her to a closed door that had brass bolts top and bottom. He slid these back, then reached up to the ledge above the architrave, but immediately froze. "The key's gone! Elsie?" He turned to his wife, but she'd disappeared. Mr D then gave the doorknob an experimental twist. To his surprise, it gave. The door swung outwards, wrong-footing Susan who, lost for words, found herself gazing at Jenny's clothing. "May I?" said Mr Duxbury, gently reaching in and pushing some coat hangers aside. Susan saw Jenny's room from a new perspective. She'd left the wardrobe doors open, she realised.

"I suppose we've some explaining to do," continued Mr Duxbury, turning back towards Susan.

He carefully bolted the door and led her back downstairs. This time she did accept a cup of coffee. She felt in need of caffeine. As they stood together in the kitchen, he assured Susan that his wife would have returned to bed. He explained about her "sundowning", a condition which meant that she became agitated at night and often wandered about.

He was profusely apologetic about his wife's invasion of Susan's property. "We've *always* kept that door locked, but Elsie must have found the key."

Mr Duxbury went on to explain that his wife had grown up in the house. "The flying freehold was then held in this – er, our half of the property. Elsie grew up in that room. The one that's now Jenny's. There was no wardrobe then, just a doorway. My wife hated it when the Oldhams relegated her room to a storage area. So, when she saw Jenny arrive, she was delighted."

"But who is Wendy?" interrupted Susan.

"Ah!" Mr D took a deep breath to steady himself. "Wendy is – or rather was – Elsie's cousin. Their family used to live in the other half – your half. It was Wendy who had Jenny's room before it became Elsie's."

"So …," began Susan, after a long silence during which Mr D busied himself with the coffee.

"Unfortunately," he finally went on, handing her a cup as they made themselves comfortable at the kitchen table, "the child developed meningitis, spending long periods isolated in that room until … she died."

There was another, respectful silence. "So that means," said Susan, picking up the thread, "that Jenny's imaginary friend is …" She petered out, not sure how to continue.

Eventually Mr D spoke again, "I must apologise for my wife's wandering. It has become worse recently. For some reason she seems more anxious and agitated. I think she feels proprietorial about her old room. She'd become an adult by the time she left it. That's when the wardrobe was built and the flying freehold became official, with lawyers involved."

His voice wavered slightly. "We never needed that room because we couldn't have children. Elsie's spinal injury, you know. She had a bad fall when she was a child – an accident, tumbling out of that old apple tree of ours."

Mr Duxbury was just becoming more expansive when Susan heard Richard's car in the drive. She was annoyed but had little option other than to conclude their chat. She was also keen to update Richard before Jenny returned from school.

This said, she'd barely managed to greet Richard before Mr D was standing alongside them in their driveway. He was holding up the lost key, impressing on them that it would never again fall into his wife's hands.

Richard was perplexed by what was going on. However, he seized the moment to ask if he could erect some scaffolding on Mr D's side of the fence, to repair Jenny's window-frame. Mr D readily agreed, once more expressing regret about the unfortunate misadventure of Mr Oldham.

When Mr D had left, Susan hastily explained about Elsie's nocturnal appearance through the wardrobe in Jenny's room. As Susan emphasised, though, the elephant in the room was not Elsie, but Wendy. She explained about this deceased cousin, finishing with the bombshell she'd just heard from their neighbour. It was not just that Mrs D had a crooked back after a childhood fall from their apple tree, but that she'd fallen after someone had told her she could fly!

Soon after, Jenny came home from school, and it wasn't long before her parents were cautioning her against any flying ventures, either alone or with friends (and this, they stressed, included "imaginary" friends). Susan was also aware that she'd no longer be sleeping alongside Jenny, keeping an eye on her, but she was determined to check up on her regularly – and, just as regularly, to check up on the wardrobe.

❨❄❩

It was about two weeks later that matters came to a head. By then, Susan was at her wits' end. As if conscious of her fragile state, the window frame in Jenny's room had begun rattling more persistently. Richard had managed to get a local firm to erect some scaffolding, but Susan, whose paranoia about poltergeists was growing, was pursuing a different course. She was trying to find a local medium.

It wasn't just the window frame that disturbed her, as she told Richard. Some mornings Jenny's toys were still to be found scattered over her bedroom floor, despite

Mrs Duxbury's nocturnal intrusions being curbed. The worst time had been when the pieces to Jenny's jigsaws were all mixed-up in a pile on her carpet.

Susan was loath to question her daughter too closely, wary of causing emotional distress. Still, there were a number of matters eating away at Susan. Was Jenny causing these events, deliberately or unconsciously, or was it something external? Or, even more disturbingly, was something supernatural operating through Jenny? How, too, had her daughter come up with the name "Wendy"? Had it come from *Peter Pan*, or from Wendy herself? Or, had Mrs Duxbury mentioned the cousin's name to Jenny?

Lying there, on yet another sleepless night, Susan turned over these matters as she again watched the darkness pale into day. Suddenly, she heard Jenny scream. Waking Richard, they both ran to Jenny's room where they found their daughter, nightdress billowing, leaning halfway out of her window. Beyond her, they could discern a figure who appeared to be floating in the air like a demon. It was only after a few seconds of abject horror that Susan remembered the scaffolding out there. And, on it, enticing Jenny to go for a flight – or so it seemed – was Mrs Duxbury.

Jenny continued to scream as Susan and Richard stood either side of her, holding on to her legs while trying to free her from Mrs D's clutches. As for Mrs D herself, there was a disturbing vacancy in her eyes, as though she was still asleep. Her lips were twitching compulsively as she mumbled to herself. Susan thought she caught the word Wendy, but it might equally have been windy, which it certainly was.

The scaffolding was creaking and groaning and, now and again, emitting a plaintive sigh as the wind played over the metal poles' open ends. It was as though a giant flautist were practising his scales.

Then Susan became aware that both she and Richard were yelling. Curiously, given her situation, only Mrs Duxbury seemed relatively quiet. Susan watched as the woman's long white hair, usually worn in a bun, blew freely round her head. Rather than making her look more haggard and demonic, it seemed to hide her wrinkles, and she appeared younger, almost childlike. She also seemed to be smiling for once.

Whenever Susan thought back on that night, it was the moments of stillness that came to mind. It was perplexing, for things were generally frenetic as she and Richard struggled to keep hold of Jenny, trying to drag her back through the window and break Mrs D's iron grip. In Susan's mind, they were struggling like that for an age until, all of a sudden, it was over. She, Richard and Jenny fell back into the bedroom. Before they could pick themselves up from the bedroom floor and go to her aid, Mrs D had disappeared from view. They distinctly heard her departing words, "Come, Wendy. Time to go." There followed a high-pitched wail, abruptly curtailed by a sickening thud.

"Oh, Elsie," they heard Mr Duxbury's voice float up from below.

Leaving Jenny with Richard, Susan ran down to him, standing over Elsie's broken body.

He explained that he'd heard his wife leave the house. "Since she lost that key, she's been desperate to find a way back into Jenny's room. I gave chase but when she's manic, she's the energy of a child."

Given her terrible fall, she looked surprisingly peaceful, Susan thought.

☽❋☾

No one was ever certain about what had occurred that night, although, between them, they shared their varying perspectives. Of course, they'd also had to share their accounts with the police, and then there were the neighbours, the press and the media, all keen to know what had gone on.

Somehow, they got through it. Susan's main concern was always Jenny, though their daughter seemed to have emerged with remarkable resilience. It was she, in fact, who put them right on a few matters.

For a start, Jenny insisted that Mrs D had climbed the scaffolding not to remove her, but Wendy. Mrs D had told Jenny that her cousin needed to leave. Also, according to Jenny, Mrs D had not been trying to drag Jenny onto the scaffolding. As Susan understood it, Mrs D was simply trying to pull Jenny beyond the confines of the room in order to free her from Wendy's clutches.

"That," Jenny had told her mother, "was when Wendy let go of me. Then they flew off together."

Susan did not correct Jenny on this last point. Both she and Richard had shielded their daughter from Mrs D's fate, only telling her much later that their elderly neighbour had died after a fall.

Although it was way out of her comfort zone, Susan slowly came round to the view that Mrs D had always had Jenny's interests at heart – even when she'd invaded Jenny's room. The old woman had been trying to protect Jenny from Wendy. Had Elsie not, from personal experience, learnt how possessive and dangerous her cousin was? She had, after all, carried the scars for most of her life, ever since she'd been persuaded that she could fly from the top of the apple tree.

Mr Duxbury, whilst understandably grief-stricken, was thankful that Elsie's life had ended at her beloved childhood home, rather than in some anonymous nursing institution. This, anyway, was what he'd said at her funeral.

❄

There were no more flying lessons in Jenny's room and Wendy was never mentioned again. Lucy, from *The Lion, the Witch and the Wardrobe*, was now Jenny's favourite, though not as an imaginary friend. It was just that Jenny and her pals – her flesh-and-blood pals

– found this room, with its magical wardrobe, the best place to play their Narnia games.

Susan and Richard were fully aware that the wardrobe really was a portal to another realm, but they decided not to tell Jenny this. It could wait until old Mr Duxbury was no longer around. Then, once again, it would be something for the lawyers to sort out.

Ghosties in the Machine

"**D**id you feel that weird sensation at the top of The Shambles?" I began, but Peter interrupted me.

"Another round?"

The three of us nodded. We were in the Bark and Quack, officially the Dog and Duck. I'd just fronted my first "Ghosties" tour: up the Shambles and across the road to York Minster. Previously I'd only done bit parts: dressing up, moaning and generally scaring people. But the others – Steve, Peter and Mark, who'd

been running the tours since they'd left drama school –
had thought I was ready for more. They also thought a
female might pull in more punters. Between ourselves,
the tour was known as "The Shambolic", which it was
in more ways than one. No one was ever quite sure
what was going to happen, or who might pull a stunt.
It kept us on our toes.

I'm biased, but I thought my tour a great success. It
had a different feel, though I can't really take the credit
for that. There was something strange going on at the
top of the Shambles, something weird and magical that
I hadn't experienced before; something that I thought
was mirrored in the eyes of the audience.

While Peter was at the bar, Steve was getting
increasingly techie. He was trying to work out how to
stage the illusion of some Roman soldiers marching,
visible only from the knees up, for this was how the
most famous ghosts in York were said to appear in the
cellars of the Treasurer's House (since the old Roman
road sat about half a metre lower down).

We groaned as Steve detailed the oscillating
frequencies of strobe lighting. Mark got up to poke the
fire. He and Steve were an item. I'd met them through
Peter. We had once been together, but it hadn't worked
out. We were still friends, though, and I'd been allowed
to keep my room in their communal house.

I again started to describe the weird sensation
everyone had experienced at the top of the Shambles,

but my remarks were lost as Peter returned with the latest round of drinks.

"Did you see how the audience were dressed tonight?" he said, passing glasses. "Impressive or what?"

"Yeah, some great costumes," said Mark. "Almost upstaged us."

Ghosties had developed a reputation for having people dress up for their tours. Our website features many of their get-ups in the hope that future punters might be inspired.

We tried to theme our tours, too, highlighting particular historical periods. Tonight was meant to be Elizabethan, but the audience were an anachronistic bunch, dressed mainly in Victorian and Medieval outfits, with a few eccentric Romans and one lone Viking. However, as I always maintain, anachronism is a meaningless concept for ghosts, for that's just what they are: beings out of time. I'd worked this up into quite a spiel. According to Peter, rather too much so!

"Apart from that boring-looking couple," said Steve, "everyone was in costume tonight."

"Who *were* those two, anyway?" asked Peter. "They always stood apart from the rest."

"Well, it's funny you should ask, Peter, because one of them," Steve paused, "dropped this." He passed Peter a business card.

"Time-Machine Tours," Peter read out. "Visit your Favourite Historical Era! Experience Genuine Period

Shopping!" He studied the card for a few moments before a smile spread across his face. "Whose brainwave was this?"

"What do you mean?" said Steve, all innocence. It took a while for him to come clean. "Good one, eh?" he smiled. "We could work it into the tours, yeah? For that extra *dimension*?"

"And while we're discussing set-ups, who was the Viking?" I asked. The others denied any knowledge. "Come on. He can't have been for real, spouting that Noggin the Nog gobbledegook."

But the others were intransigent. So I once more mentioned the elephant in the room. "Didn't you feel it? That shuddery sensation at the top of the Shambles?"

"You don't mean that man who came out of the alley with the meat cleaver, dripping blood?" said Steve.

"No, I don't!" I knew Steve was peeved that I'd not yet mentioned his unscheduled appearance, terrifying us all. "I knew it was you. I recognised the trainers." My eyes travelled down to his feet. No trainers! "But it *was* you," I stumbled on.

"What, these trainers?" Steve pulled them from a carrier bag while the others hooted. "Got you there!"

I said no more until we were back at the house, sitting over coffee. Just as I was about to mention the ghosty in our machine again, Peter's mobile rang. "It's the Viking," he said, passing me the phone.

I could see the others sniggering. I *had* been set up! Sven, as he was called, had agreed to play the Viking in exchange for an introduction. I was not in the mood. However, before I hung up, I impulsively asked him if he'd experienced anything strange at the top of the Shambles.

I put the phone on speaker: "… there was certainly a … coldness. A walking-over-grave feeling – is that how you say it? Very realistic illusion."

I thanked Sven and, after promising him I'd be in touch, hung up.

"See?" I said. "Punter feedback."

"It was quite windy out there," conceded Steve. The others nodded.

"No!" I protested. "It was on the inside. In your guts. Like something had passed through you and rattled your ribcage." Still nothing. "You could see the shock register on the punters' faces – like Noggin's, I mean Sven's."

But the three wise monkeys kept shtum.

"Maybe," suggested Peter, "it was those Roman soldiers marching past."

The others laughed. I felt like I was competing with Blackpool illuminations by waving my lone candle in the air.

"Speaking of the soldier idea," said Steve, "how about, alongside the shop fronts, we have a bit of cloth stretched across – about knee height – painted the same as the bits of shopfront they're concealing? A couple of us then walk behind that false front, dressed as Romans, so our legs below the knee are hidden."

"That's it" said Peter. "And we could light it with a strobe."

I got up, leaving the boys to their smoke and mirrors. "With you lot around, no supernatural phenomenon stands a chance," I shouted from the door.

There was silence until I was about halfway up the stairs, when Steve's portable wind machine – cleverly concealed behind the landing curtains – kicked in, wrenching an involuntary scream from me.

Below, raucous laughter erupted from the lads.

Boys and their toys. I didn't stand a chance!

The Ghostwriter

I

Life had been going well for Sam Worth. After he'd left the soap, *Upton Village*, he'd had a successful run in a West End play and was now being offered more serious roles. Ever since performing in school plays, it had been his dream to be on stage. However, he'd been told by his manager, Karl Crowther, that the day job wasn't enough. He should be on chat shows, in adverts and celebrating his achievements on social media.

To those in the know, Karl was regarded as the English Colonel Parker. The reference was lost on Sam. "Elvis Presley's Svengali," people explained, but Svengali also had to be spelled out to Sam. Although he did recall being referred to as Karl's "golden goose". Perhaps that's when Sam's doubts began, doubts that grew as Karl badgered him to write something, "like a children's book, or a memoir maybe."

For highly personal reasons, Sam had taken exception, confessing that he was seriously dyslexic. Karl had simply laughed, which shocked Sam. Nowadays, Sam thought, no one made fun of such a disability. Regardless of his protestations though, Karl persisted with the idea.

"Don't worry, son," he assured his protégé. "We have people to do the heavy lifting. Ghostwriters."

Sam did not like the sound of that. He pictured a skeletal figure, like Marley's ghost. But after being introduced to Tom Graham, Sam was put at ease. Tom explained the process: how Sam just needed to talk about his growing up and Tom would then shape what he'd said into a lively narrative. "I'm merely a midwife, or ghost," Tom assured him. "The book will appear under your name."

"But that's dishonest," protested Sam.

"That's the ghostwriter's lot," answered Tom. "Just think of me as your amanuensis."

"A man who … what?"

"Sorry," said Tom. "It's a fancy word for a secretary. I suffer from the opposite affliction to you. *Logophilia*, a love of words."

Sam shook his head. He was pleasantly surprised to discover how much he enjoyed his get-togethers with Tom. In a world of glitzy madness, their meetings proved to be rare moments of sanity. The two made good progress.

Then suddenly the get-togethers came to an end after a devastating fire at Tom's house. It was said that had the writer not spent time trying to rescue his precious manuscripts – including material for the proposed *Book of Sam*, as Tom called it – he might have escaped.

Sam was bereft, and he felt guilty, especially after the police interviewed him, despite their assurance it was just a formality. Karl's reaction also surprised him. Usually, his manager turned any chance of publicity into a media circus, but on this occasion he was uncharacteristically reticent.

2

Karl knew he'd hit gold when he discovered Sam. He'd had to see off a few competitors before he managed to sign the lad, but that was nothing new. All had gone well until that ghostwriter had started asking questions. Not that Tom would unearth any dirt about Sam. The lad was squeaky clean. Maybe he'd occasionally inhaled a joint, but that was about it.

Karl realised that he should have found out more about Tom Graham before hiring him. He subsequently discovered that the man had been an investigative journalist, which didn't bode well. Karl then warned his boys against talking to Graham, with whom Karl had a personal word. "Stick to Sam's story and leave mine alone," he'd suggested.

Such talk must only have whetted Tom's appetite. Through his boys, Karl learnt that the ghostwriter now knew quite a lot about his past: that he was formerly Carl Lowther (not a very imaginative change), a man involved in drug trafficking, pimping and protection racketeering. It was at this point that Karl had decided a fire was necessary. The coroner's verdict cited a faulty boiler as the cause.

After this "accident", Karl shelved Sam's memoir and, given the time of year, booked some singing lessons for his protégé with a view to Sam making a Christmas album. It would open up work in musicals.

☾✱☽

About a month after the fire, Karl received a strange phone call. He'd been out jogging, something that he'd taken up after a recent TIA. His doctor had told him to mend his ways, or else. Jogging had seemed the least unattractive option to Karl, who didn't intend putting his flabby self on display at any gym or pool. So, wearing his tracksuit with the hood up, Karl started taking a few leisurely laps round his local park while listening to the latest Lee Child on Audible. It was on one of these occasions that a phone call interrupted Jack Reacher's exploits.

Karl stopped to look at the caller ID. It was his mother! Since she'd been put in a home, she never rang. He answered, "Ma?"

"Is that you, Karl?" her voice came shakily through his earbuds.

"Ma?" he said again, pushing back his hood and wiping the sweat from his brow. She was incapable of using a phone, surely, let alone remembering she had a son.

"There's someone here wants a word. Will you take the call?"

It was a strange thing to say, thought Karl, but then it was his mother being, for her, reasonably lucid.

"Sure thing, Ma. Put 'em on."

There was a brief clicking before a male voice spoke. "I'm glad you invited me in, Karrrl."

Must be a doctor, thought Karl. "Who's that speaking? And 'let you in' *where*, exactly?"

"Into your head, Karrrl. You *invited* me in. Remember that."

Karl disliked the way the man pronounced his name, with a real lip curl. "Nutter!" was his one-word reply before terminating the call.

He went back to Jack Reacher. But after another lap of the park, he realised he'd not heard a word. In his head, that voice still resounded: "Karrrl!"

He went home and took a shower, giving his ears a good scour, as though to rid himself of that intrusive speaker.

The rest of the day Karl spent trying to find a singing coach for Sam. Normally, he'd have allotted this task to someone else, but today he wanted to keep busy. It was only towards evening that he let himself relax with a glass of Bell's. He was dozing off when he heard that voice again.

"Karrrl!"

He woke with a start, scrabbling for his phone, thinking he must have dropped it in his armchair. Then he realised that the voice was coming from *inside* his head. He tried turning up the volume on his TV to drown it out, but it was no good. He reached for his whisky and slopped the liquid down his shirt.

"You're not answering me, Karrrl … so we've got a long night ahead."

"Bullshit!" said Karl, striving to gain the upper hand.

"You remember me? The one you *incinerated?*" Karl winced. "Tom Graham, your ghostwriter, now," the voice chuckled, "fully-qualified."

"Stop pissing about, Tom Graham's …"

"Dead. Yes, Karrrl. Dead. And we know who's responsible, don't we?"

"I didn't do it!"

"No. You *had* it done. It's a bit like ghostwriting, isn't it? Doing something on someone's behalf."

Karl said nothing.

"Didn't like what I discovered, did you, *Carl Lowther*?"

Karl remained silent.

"So, I'm no longer Sam's ghostwriter. I'm yours now. Exclusively. Your resident ghost, or host if you'd prefer."

Karl still said nothing.

"Well, I'll leave you to your whisky. Try not to spill any more."

Karl spilled a good deal more, but most of it down his throat until it eventually rendered him unconscious.

In the morning, Karl tried to laugh it off and blamed the drink. Ghosts, indeed! They didn't behave like that, did they? They made screechy noises and paraded around. That was the point of them, wasn't it? Apparitions. Also, of course, they turned out to be people, didn't they, dressed up in sheets, like on *Scooby Doo*, or like the Klan?

But try as he might, Karl couldn't escape the feeling that someone else was in his head. While going about his business, he made an effort to guard his thoughts, worried about what he might be giving away. In meetings, he found himself pausing, mid-sentence, to listen out for an eavesdropper. This went on for several days. His staff became increasingly concerned that their boss was losing it, that his drinking was getting the upper hand. Then, just as Karl began to relax his guard, to feel that this ghost, or host (or whatever), must have been some sort of hallucination, it popped up again.

"Boo!" it said.

Karl thought he was experiencing his second TIA. His body jackknifed in shock. He'd planned to ignore the voice if it returned, but he found it very difficult to do so. He tried turning up his TV; then tried putting in his earbuds and filling his head with AC/DC. However, despite him singing along loudly to "Highway to Hell" the ghostwriter still penetrated. "Good choice," it said. After this, Karl hit the whisky with vehemence, listening only half-heartedly to the voice reminding him of highlights from his past. Once again, unconsciousness finally liberated him.

The following morning, apart from the self-inflicted clanging and banging inside his head, Karl thought he was alone. He was appalled at the detail the ghostwriter had dug up about him, going back to his early drug-pushing and pimping days.

The next week was a nightmare. He couldn't concentrate on anything, always on edge, dreading the voice's next interjection. As the days passed, he almost wished it would declare itself as the silence was becoming increasingly ominous. He tried to pursue his "normal" business, but he knew he was distracted, not thinking straight, and his staff seemed to know it, too. They began to treat him like a disturbed child, and he was aware his authority was suffering.

The evenings were the worst, though, when he found himself alone. Initially, he'd tried hanging out in bars, but paranoia soon overtook him, and he narrowly avoided several fights. "Who you looking at, pal?" just didn't cut it when the eyeballer was on the inside. After that, he took to drinking at home, on his own, but the dread of "the voice" was even worse there. In the end, he invited over one of his girls, Sonya, to keep him company.

They'd had a pizza delivered and were drinking cocktails, half-heartedly watching one of Karl's less hardcore movies. Karl had warned Sonya that, if he should behave strangely, she was not to worry. But Karl was thinking only of that voice resounding within his head, not expecting hammy Hammer Horror effects. It was as though the ghostwriter was determined to display his credentials as a bona fide spirit.

First, there came the relatively subtle billowing of his curtains.

"Oh, come on," said Karl, who was feeling quite bullish with Sonya beside him, "You can do better than that, surely?"

"What you on about, Karl?" Sonya asked, lifting her nose from her Prosecco. "You're twitchy tonight."

"The curtains," he replied. "Didn't you see them blowing?"

"There's no wind, Karl, and that window's shut."

"No wind! Can't you hear it in the chimney?" Karl raised his hand, as though to mute the sound of the movie, but then the lounge door creaked loudly. "And look," he said, pointing towards the door, which was slowly swinging ajar.

"What now?"

"Can't you see it?" Karl's gestures were increasingly histrionic as he watched the door creak shut again, as though proving the wind wasn't the cause.

"For God's sake, Karl. I'd lay off the juice if I were you," said Sonya, quaffing more Prosecco.

Karl flopped back on the settee. He now knew it was all in his head, which was in line with what he'd googled earlier: "Auditory and visual hallucinations are relatively common, but if the voices start talking about aliens or ordering you to kill people, report to your GP immediately."

Next thing, Karl felt his left hand twinge. He looked down and watched it arch into a claw, his finger ends fastening over the rim of his whisky tumbler. He'd no idea what his hand was up to. He seemed to have lost control of it, as he realised when he tried to withdraw it. His attempts became more frantic as he watched his finger ends push themselves down inside the rim of the glass, catching his fingernails on the outside. His fingers, he realised, were methodically prising the nails from their beds. He roared with pain.

"What is *wrong* with you?" demanded Sonya as she lifted his hand, with seeming ease, from the glass.

Karl was whimpering now. It was at this moment that the voice returned, whispering, "That was nothing, Karrrl. Imagine that level of pain going on for an eternity. We don't need red-hot pincers to wrench out your tongue, or metal tongs to blister your flesh." The voice paused before adding, "Though none of it is as bad as being burned alive."

Karl gulped.

"Your mum's a lovely lady, by the way. I'm glad we could trace her."

Sonya was studying Karl's hand. "There's nothing here. Was it cramp, perhaps?"

"Leave me alone," Karl yelled at Tom.

"Well, thank you *very* much!" said Sonya, getting up and flouncing out of the room. "I'm getting a taxi."

"No, I didn't mean you, doll," shouted Karl.

But she'd gone. Karl grunted and, once again, sought succour in whisky. It was obvious that these things were happening only inside his head, even though the pain was eye-watering. But Karl was relatively inured to pain. It had been the currency of his upbringing: beatings, dousings, burnings and the like. That said, the way the ghostwriter had taken control of Karl's body didn't seem quite fair. He worried about what might be coming next.

Immediately this thought crossed his mind, he clamped a hand over his mouth – as though this action would prevent the ghostwriter from eavesdropping. "Knobhead!" he berated himself.

Eventually, Karl started making his wobbly way to bed. But, when he reached the top of the stairs, his legs marched him in the wrong direction, to the big landing window. He knew he couldn't blame the drink for this. He cursed himself for being so open with his thoughts earlier – as if that had made any difference.

Next thing Karl knew, he was flinging wide the casement window and clambering onto the sill. He found himself gazing down at the distant pavement.

It seemed an age that he stood there, swaying in the breeze (so there was a breeze after all, he noted), unable to move. Eventually, he could bear it no longer. "Come on, then," he shouted. "Do it if you're going to! Or haven't you the balls? You've certainly got mine!"

The ghostwriter broke his silence. "You've just made me realise. I'm starting to play it your way, aren't I? Intimidation? Scare tactics? But I'm not going to descend to your level – which, by the way, lies far below that pavement." There was a pause. "No. Unlike you, I like to think I still have a moral compass."

"Yeah! Bet you were in the Boy Scouts, too," Karl sneered. He suddenly felt cocky, as though he'd finally got the measure of his tormenter. He'd dealt with middle-class wankers like Tom before.

His cockiness waned as the ghostwriter continued, "So we're going to help you take responsibility for your actions. That is, 'rehabilitate' you. Turn you into someone who really cares."

"Jesus, can't you talk the talk!" said Karl. "Who do you think I am? Some character from one of your poncy books?"

The ghostwriter didn't rise to this, but went on, "Perhaps a few years inside will help you see the error of your ways. Let you come to terms with yourself."

Inside was not a word Karl liked to hear. It wasn't doing the porridge that worried him, it was the claustrophobia of the place. Then, as Karl once again realised, he was thinking too openly. "Minds have ears," he reminded himself.

❈

It didn't seem more than a few minutes before Karl's alarm went off, except that it rang only in his head. Like a condemned man he clambered out of bed, not sure whose volition he was under. The ghostwriter was certainly keeping mum, despite Karl's attempts to provoke a response. "What you doing pal, this time of night?"

Once dressed, Karl found himself walking into his office, switching on his computer and opening a Word document.

"Confession," he found himself typing, after which his fingers sped up. Karl couldn't believe how fast they raced over the keyboard. He could hardly read that fast. But he did see enough to get the drift of this "confession". He recognised the names of victims and accomplices, the bank account numbers and so on. Finally, Tom Graham's name flashed up, alongside the name of the arsonist, Kenny Wall.

The next thing Karl found himself doing was printing, signing, scanning and, finally, forwarding this document to the police.

It was still morning when there was a knock at the door.

3

Prison certainly cured Karl of his claustrophobia. Involuntarily, he experienced a therapy known as "flooding". But that wasn't the only thing that had changed about Karl. Those who visited him were amazed at the transformation. For those who believed in the rehabilitatory potential of prison, Karl was a shining example.

Sam was certainly impressed. For the last seven years, he'd managed to concentrate on his acting and his career had gone from strength to strength. He'd starred in a few films and earned some prestigious awards. He still found time to visit Karl, despite the terrible things he'd learnt about his former manager. Sam kept Karl abreast of his successes.

What surprised Sam was the genuine interest Karl now showed in his protégé's acting. He even helped Sam learn his lines, prompting when necessary. Karl particularly liked to hear Sam deliver the big soliloquies from Shakespeare, and Sam certainly enjoyed performing them.

Even more surprising was Karl's new-found interests, not just in reading but also in writing. The two shared books and discussed favourite authors. Sam was still behoven to Tom for opening up this world to him, and he habitually sang his praises. Strangely, Karl did not seem to mind hearing the ghostwriter's name lauded. He seemed to accept his guilt responsibly.

On his most recent visit Karl had once again surprised Sam by handing the actor a manuscript, announcing, "My autobiography."

Sam found it unexpectedly candid. After detailing his tough upbringing and subsequent career as a drug dealer, loan shark, pimp and, of course, impresario, it seemed that Karl had undergone a miraculous conversion.

"I found my moral compass," Karl had written, "when I sent that confession to the police." It was no wonder he was recommended for early release. He was a shining example for the criminal justice system to champion.

Several other sentences in Karl's autobiography leapt out at Sam, but it was these lines he found especially intriguing:

> I know many people employ a
> ghostwriter to write their memoirs.
> Originally, I'd planned to do the
> same but, over time, and with the
> prison library at my disposal, I'd
> come to feel confident enough to
> write my own. In fact, I've become
> a complete logophile. I feel like a
> new man!

The Night Mare

I woke to feel something squatting on my chest. It was too heavy for the cat but as I always sleep in complete darkness (I have blackout curtains as any light disturbs me), I wasn't sure what it was.

Why didn't I reach out and dislodge it, you might be wondering. I felt paralysed, that's why. My arms were trapped beneath the bedclothes. Beyond that, I was concerned about "the thing". It whimpered like an orphaned child.

"Are you alright?" I eventually asked, my voice sounding more alien than anything else in that black room.

The creature froze, I could sense it. And, as I lay there, I remember thinking, if it is an animal, the last thing I want to hear is an answer! Just as I'd decided that it must indeed be a brute beast, a thin, high-pitched voice broke the silence.

"I'm lonely," it said.

That was all, and in such perfect English, with no discernible accent, that after a while I wondered whether it had spoken at all. Perhaps it had communicated telepathically? Or perhaps I was dreaming – hallucinating, even? Then the sobbing began again and I was shaken out of my comatose reverie.

"Come on," I said, "get it off your chest." Immediately I'd spoken, I wanted to laugh, my remark sounding so unexpectedly apposite. However, I couldn't rise to the occasion for my lungs were constricted by my visitor. "And, please," I eventually gasped, "get off my chest. I can hardly breathe."

The creature moved over, but only to squat beside me. The relief was intense. My lungs grabbed the fresh air. I was also able to liberate my arms.

"I like to feel people breathe," it added.

I could now indulge in a laugh. "But you make it so difficult!"

"I know," it sniffed. "But breathing and heartbeats … they're such a comfort."

I was now quite awake. I puffed my pillows and raised myself on my elbows.

"What *are* you?"

I had no truck with the supernatural, but this creature seemed obdurately physical.

"I've been called many things."

"Where have you come from? And how did you get here?" My questions gained momentum.

It took a while, but eventually the creature explained that it had "no place" to come from. It migrated from one sleeping body to another – man, woman, Russian, Arab, Eskimo … whoever. It was known by various names: Basty, Tokoloshe, Tsog Tsuam, Old Hag, Incubus, Mare. These are the only ones I can recall. None of them, the creature added, were respectful.

Once again, it proclaimed its loneliness, being the only one of its kind – or so it thought. For centuries it had searched for a kindred spirit. Unfortunately, though it craved company and warmth, it elicited only terror and hysteria, being repeatedly spurned and driven away. Few people showed compassion, it said, thanking me for my sympathetic forbearance.

I was now even more curious to know what sort of creature I was talking to. I asked if I might turn on the light, but the very idea elicited panic.

"Light … hurts," the creature said and took my hand. Its touch was icy but not otherwise unpleasant. It guided my fingers to what I presume was its chest, which also felt glacial (and, as far as I could tell, without a heartbeat). The skin was ridged and scaly.

"Light burns!" it emphasised.

I assured the creature there would be no light.

"Thank you," it said. "Your kindness means a great deal."

I'd like to tell you more about my mysterious, nocturnal visitor. I had many more questions but, all of a sudden, I felt inordinately tired. I have a recollection that the word "sleep" was being intoned, but whether this incantation (for so it seemed) came from the creature or from my own weary brain, I cannot be sure. I also recall a heavy scent pervading the air. But again, I might be mistaken. All I really know is that I slept through the rest of the night, to wake refreshed. For me, this was most unusual.

Almost needless to say, I awoke alone.

❨❀❩

Since that night I have often puzzled over my experience. Was it simply a dream? After all, I have no evidence of any visitation. But, although a dream is the obvious explanation, I cannot quite accept it. The experience felt too real and has haunted me ever since. There are also those names that the creature mentioned, most of which I'm sure I'd never heard before. And yet, I have since discovered that these names are real.

I must also mention the shock of encountering Henry Fuseli's famous artwork, *The Nightmare*. Was this the same creature that visited me? Had Fuseli, perhaps, illuminated the creature in order to paint it? Had this, perhaps, been the cause of its burns?

That said, Fuseli's image diverges from my own in several regards. Those large, pointed ears and bulging eyeballs, let alone that thickset, porcine appearance, seem all wrong. Fuseli also has that gormless horse peering round a curtain, although the word "mare" – of Old English origin, apparently – has nothing equine about it. It is simply a term for an evil spirit, although my visitor was hardly that!

My nocturnal creature was an innocent, I'm sure of it. Someone to be pitied rather than reviled, doomed to shift location each night, forever an outcast.

I should add that, although I have used the neuter pronoun in this account, "it" sounds demeaning. Yet I don't know how otherwise to designate my visitor. Does s/he, in fact, have a sex? Though fanciful, I do like to think that, one day, "it" might encounter another of its kind.

I wish the creature would revisit. On the off chance, I now leave my window ajar. Of course, if anyone else has encountered this benighted creature, please, do get in touch.

Strait is the Gate

"Spaghetti Junction," said Howard, picturing the cars as bits of mince trapped in an endless tangle of pasta.

He was making his way home after an exhausting week at the Bristol office. Spaghetti Junction swooped above and below him. The traffic was ridiculous, thought Howard; although, as his car doubled as his office, he felt more entitled to be on the road than most.

"What's that, Mr Welby?" came a voice from his car speaker.

"Oh nothing, Mr Johnson," spluttered Howard, suddenly remembering his boss was still connected. "Some obstruction on Spaghetti Junction."

"Just make sure you're back tomorrow, Welby. Good and early!" Johnson hung up.

"Yes, Mr Johnson." Howard pulled a face in his rear-view mirror. "Why don't I just go straight there now?" he asked his reflection.

There was a honking behind. Howard waved an acknowledging hand and moved up a car length.

"Driverless cars, that's what we need. Put your feet up and read."

As he left the Junction behind, overhead signs redundantly informed drivers that queues were likely and that vehicles should not travel faster than 30 mph.

"Some chance," Howard remarked to his reflection. "Never used to talk to you, did I?"

At that moment, the traffic ahead sped off. A hire truck, which had been in the lane to his right, now gathered enough momentum to swing into the impossibly tight gap that had opened in front of Howard, the vehicle's backend fishtailing menacingly. Howard, along with several other drivers, was forced to brake and swerve. Horns blared and tyres screeched.

Howard found himself unharmed, crawling along the hard shoulder, his hands welded to the steering wheel. Up ahead, he spotted a gateway with a sign that read, "No Entry for Motorway Traffic". Howard, reluctant to fight his way back onto the motorway, ignored the sign and slipped through the forbidden opening.

His car climbed over a gentle rise and descended into some scrubby woodland beyond. Immediately, he felt his stress levels subside. The noise of the motorway magically segued into birdsong and, as he slipped the car into neutral, he thought he could hear sheep bleating in the distance. The patchwork of fields that lay before him took him straight back to childhood: holidaying in remote farmhouses in North Wales; chasing lackadaisical streams to discover where they bubbled up, distinctively Welsh in their lilt.

He encountered a slight gradient and slipped the car back into gear and, breasting the rise, a farmhouse came into view. He headed for it, though why this should be his destination, he had no idea.

As he drew closer to the farm, a man stepped onto the track. Howard recalled the "No Entry" sign. The man was dressed casually in corduroy trousers and a sports jacket.

"I think I must have taken a wrong turn," Howard confessed through his open window.

"No bother," replied the man, in an accent Howard couldn't quite place. "Where you headed?"

"Far from the madding crowd," said Howard. For no apparent reason, some lines from Gray's *Elegy*, learnt back in childhood, had sprung into his head.

"Then bide a while," said the man. "Leave your car here."

"That's very decent of you," Howard said, uncurling his hands from the steering wheel.

The man led him round the back of the farmhouse into an old-fashioned kitchen with a range on one side and cupboards and dressers occupying the other walls. A large oak table stood in the middle, at which a woman, about the same age as the man, was mixing something in a large bowl.

"Found this chap outside, Maggie. Thought he'd like a cuppa."

"Why, of course, Albert," she said, dropping her wooden spoon into the bowl and moving across to the range, where a kettle steamed expectantly.

Soon all three of them were sitting round the table, as though Howard were a neighbour who had just popped in. Next to his mug of tea was a plate heaped with slices of fruit cake and slabs of crumbly white cheese. He hadn't meant to have any, but it smelt so delicious, and his hosts were already tucking in.

Not only was the cake their own but so was the cheese, he learnt. It melted in his mouth as soon as it touched his tongue. Howard was told that the family had been there for several generations, farming the area long before the combustion engine ruled the land.

After the tea, Albert gave Howard a tour. Before he knew it, an hour had passed. Howard tried to ring Eileen, his wife, but could get no signal, and Albert and Maggie had no house phone.

The next minute, Albert and Maggie were standing on the porch, waving goodbye. He must have driven like an automaton because, the next thing he knew, he was home, greeting Eileen.

"You're whistling," she noted. "Haven't heard you whistle in years."

"So I am," he replied, "Welby by name …"

"And well-be by nature!"

They laughed at their old joke.

Howard passed her a bunch of carnations – an unusual gift from him, considering it wasn't her birthday – and told her about his adventures. He felt like a schoolkid returning from playing in the park. But as he spoke, he realised he'd hardly asked Albert and Maggie anything about themselves.

✸

From that day, life seemed to change for Howard. His boss, Mr Johnson, was soon to be sacked for bullying. Nothing to do with Howard, but he was the beneficiary, being promoted to Area Manager. Howard was a popular choice, too, though he maintained that anyone would have been popular after Johnson.

While Howard enjoyed his elevated status, he was surprised to discover how much he missed life on the road. Consequently, he and Eileen began to take a weekly drive on his day off, which they both enjoyed.

Their adult daughter, Katie, was more cynical about these trips, which, she said, were all about rediscovering "Maggie's Farm", as she called it (although Howard didn't approve).

"Ridiculous man!" she always declared. "He'll have had some sort of TIA and ended up on the hard shoulder, concussed and dreaming."

Eileen didn't concern herself with the cause. She was simply grateful that Howard was so happy with life, which made her happy too.

Over time, Howard talked less about "Maggie's Farm", albeit it was still on his mind. He and Eileen enjoyed six peaceful years, which had been ushered in by Johnson's departure and then consolidated by Katie's marriage. Before he knew it, Howard's own retirement came and went. Unfortunately, only three years later Eileen found she had a tumour, which proved inoperable. Their time together was suddenly precious.

When Eileen became bedridden, Howard locked his car in the garage. This act was more symbolic than anything, for he regularly had to break it out to run errands: collecting medical supplies, taxiing relatives and friends.

On his way back from one such journey, Howard couldn't resist a detour via Spaghetti Junction. It always energised him, even though those years on the road had been frenzied, with Johnson incessantly barking in his ear. He now recalled them with affection.

When Howard shunted the vehicle in front, he was the first to admit he'd not been concentrating. Fortunately, the driver had been sympathetic, realising that Howard was a man preoccupied. As they shook hands, details exchanged, the man left Howard on the hard shoulder. Howard was meant to follow suit, but his car wouldn't start. He couldn't even open the bonnet to check why. The shunt had jammed it. He called the AA, who told him to retire behind the safety barrier and wait.

In need of a pee, Howard walked down the road to where he espied some cover. He rang Eileen to let her know about his delay, but not about the shunt.

After he'd relieved himself, he was about to return when he spotted a gateway further along. This was not unusual. Gateways beckoned wherever he went, raising his hopes that he'd rediscovered Maggie's Farm, only to find himself disappointed. However, he had time to kill, so thought he'd explore.

This time, Howard wasn't mistaken. Although in his late sixties and overweight, he broke into a run when he became convinced that this was the gateway to the fabled farm. Once more, he felt the noise of the motorway fade as the birdsong increased in volume. Tears obscured his vision. If only Eileen were here!

This time, no one met him on the drive. He went straight up to the house, making his way to the back door, where he knocked excitedly. There was no reply. "Albert? Maggie?" he called. But, apart from the country sounds – the birds, the sheep and a gentle breeze – there was only silence.

He gingerly tried the handle. The door opened and, once again, he was in that familiar kitchen, so long imprinted on his mind. The range was humming, giving the kitchen that cosy, nostalgic warmth that he had craved for so long. He was tempted to explore further but, looking at the time, he realised he should be getting back to his car and, more importantly, to Eileen. Reluctantly, he drew the door shut and retraced his steps.

As he exited the gateway, he looked back and tried to fix the spot in his mind. He returned to his car and climbed in to wait, forgetting the advice he'd been given.

A tapping noise on his window woke him: the AA, of course. The patrolman gently expressed his concern about Howard still being in his vehicle. He made Howard stand behind the barrier while he fixed his car, which only took the man a matter of minutes.

Once home, Howard quickly pulled off his coat and shouted through to Eileen. She now had her bed in the lounge, bedecked with medical equipment.

"Sorry I'm late," he apologised. "Cup of tea and I'll tell you all about it."

They sat and talked for hours. At least, Howard talked. Eileen smiled, savouring his excitement, which was itself a tonic.

The doctors and nurses thought so too, expressing great surprise, but delight as well, at Eileen's dramatic remission. She was even allowed out again, so they resumed their car journeys.

Howard thought he was being subtle, that Eileen wouldn't notice how, wherever they went, from the Cotswolds to the Forest of Dean, every journey included a detour round Spaghetti Junction. But Eileen was just happy to be alive and active.

Their relatives, too, were delighted at this new lease of life, which, they had to concede, seemed to be driven by Howard's enthusiasm for this mythical farm. No one else believed in it but, as long as it delivered its magic, they didn't really care.

Katie was the only one who persisted in puncturing her father's dreams. She'd previously confronted him with Google Maps, to prove that there were no farms in that area of motorway. Now she berated him for not securing any photographic evidence. Howard kicked himself. He'd forgotten that his phone had a camera. And why, Katie had wanted to know, hadn't he used his sat nav to get a bearing on the place?

"Twenty-first century, Dad?" she'd snorted. "And didn't the AA man *wake you at the roadside*?" Katie was very accomplished at undermining him. "Ridiculous man!" she added.

Howard held his tongue. He still maintained that Albert and Maggie's farm was out there, somewhere, and that, one day, he would find it again. He only wished Katie would have more trust in him, would indulge him in his convictions. Life, for her, sounded so grey, especially since, after a scant six months, she and her husband had separated.

Eileen's remission continued longer than anyone dared hope. She had eighteen months of good health before rapidly going downhill. It was for the best, Howard said at the funeral. He appeared remarkably sanguine about it, and everyone was impressed with his positive demeanour. Katie maintained that he'd been a different man following his promotion, although she knew full well that the main reason lay elsewhere.

After he was widowed, Howard set about redecorating the front room, and then worked his way round the rest of the house, clearing out unwanted clutter. Some thought he was simply keeping himself occupied; others, that he was preparing to put the house up for sale.

"But where will he go?" neighbours and relations asked, looking pointedly at Katie.

"No chance!" she'd assert.

Howard still had his car and kept it immaculately polished. You couldn't tell that it had been in a shunt. And he still liked to go for a drive, although the car felt dreadfully empty nowadays, despite all the solitary hours he'd spent in vehicles down the years. He explored every direction the roads would permit, but he was still drawn, inevitably, to the environs of Spaghetti Junction, its twists and loops, its highs and lows, its stops and starts.

On this particular day there were roadworks around the Junction, and Howard found himself in a long queue, the cones funnelling the vehicles from one side of the motorway to the other. He couldn't see anyone working, but that was the way, of course: cones first, repairs later.

As he sat there, he recalled his travelling days, when the heels of his shoes were always the first things to wear out. His car had been his mobile office then, its interior festooned with post-its and fast-food detritus. Crazy times!

Howard realised he hadn't been paying close attention for, as he looked about him, the congestion seemed to have dispersed. The cars ahead had pulled away without his noticing.

It was then that he saw the gateway, just the other side of a row of cones. Without considering the consequences, he swung his car through the plastic phalanx, the cones exploding in all directions, and headed for the opening, tears of joy obscuring his vision.

Once again, he experienced that magical transition as he left behind the world of the motorway. Howard slipped the car into neutral and let it glide through the farmland, listening as the birdsong took over. Sheep stopped grazing and looked up as he passed. Cows followed suit. And there, yes, there was Albert, surely, by the side of the drive, dressed as Howard remembered him: corduroy trousers, check shirt, old sports jacket.

"Hello Howard," the farmer greeted him. "Haven't seen you in a while."

"You remember me!"

"Course we do. We were expecting you."

"Really?" Howard had to wipe the tears from his face. He climbed out of his car and followed Albert round the back of the farmhouse and into the kitchen.

"You made it," said Maggie, looking up from the dough that she was kneading. The kitchen was the same. "Cup of tea?" It was as though he'd been there only last week. "Your room's ready. Show him, Albert. I need to get this in the oven."

Howard tried to protest but, on reflection, realised that he had little to go home for, and he did so love it here.

His bedroom clinched it. It was up in the eaves, with swallows swooping outside. Albert showed him round the farm again, demonstrating how things worked. And, before Howard knew it, the three of them were sitting down to dinner.

It was a steak-and-kidney pie with new potatoes, carrots and garden peas. The food was fresh and colourful, earthy with flavour. Each mouthful carried Howard further and further back into his childhood. He could still recall eating his very first meat pie: the crunch of the pastry before it dissolved on his tongue, the rich gravy oozing round his teeth.

Howard looked up at Albert and Maggie, who now reminded him of his own parents. Once he almost called Maggie "Mummy". At the end of the evening, she saw him up to his bedroom to say goodnight.

He slept peacefully and awoke fully rested, at one with the world, listening to the fledglings in the eaves. The only thing that troubled him was the thought of having to leave and return to his empty house.

He dressed and went downstairs, the smell of a fried breakfast drew him into the kitchen. He entered, ready to greet Maggie. Then he staggered, upsetting a nearby chair.

"Eileen!" he gasped. Was he still dreaming? "What are you doing here, you're …?" he couldn't bring himself to say it. Besides which, he didn't want to destroy the magic of this moment, even if it was only a dream.

"Albert and Maggie had to go away," said Eileen in a matter-of-fact way. "Long time since I've done this," she commented, loading two plates with bacon and eggs. "They asked if we'd look after the place."

"Of course," said Howard, in a daze. He would go along with anything, however bizarre. It was, after all, a dream come true. What could he say but, "You're looking well, Mrs Welby," and await her reply.

❦

Katie, who had never reverted to her more propitious maiden name, seemed to take things quite calmly when the police told her about the accident.

Her father's car, festooned in traffic cones, had been found, wedged halfway up the bank of the motorway's hard shoulder.

Katie told them that, since her mother's death, he had been putting his affairs in order, and she'd feared he might be planning something like this. "Ridiculous man!" she added.

But no sooner had she said this than her face crumpled. Her tears ran freely. The young PC looked on, embarrassed, and reached for the tissues he'd been advised to carry for such occasions.

A Tale Spinner

Never before had a tale arrived in such a finished form. Stories usually came to Mark Guthrie in dribs and drabs after a lot of painful straining. In fact, metaphors of constipation dominated. And, even then, there were still endless months of redrafting before a story felt right to him. This little gem, though, seemed to have plopped out ready-made.

Although Mark was most grateful for this gift, he was also suspicious. As he sat in the taxi on the way to Indianapolis airport, his doubts grew. Did this story actually work, or were there some glaring errors he'd yet to spot? Was it a bit sensational, the language overly demotic?

He was fully aware of what lay behind his concerns: his Irish gran. She'd been a brilliant spinner of tales. He remembered sitting round with his childhood buddies, mesmerised by her stories. It might not have been cool, but they couldn't help themselves. She had them crawling up the walls. "Go on, Gran. Go on!" they'd shout. Adults were the same, hanging on her every word. Meals would congeal and drinks turn tepid while a story unfurled. Life was put on hold.

This latest story of Mark's was certainly more like one of hers, especially in the way it had come to him. He'd had the idea while packing his bag, ready for his flight. He'd reached for his notebook before remembering his sprained right wrist. He'd grabbed his phone instead, to record the insight. However, once he'd started speaking, he found he couldn't stop. The story gushed from him. Not only that, in his lounge mirror, he'd caught glimpses of himself pulling faces and making flamboyant gestures, just as Gran used to do. Even more unnerving, he realised that the mirror in question – an ebony-framed cheval glass – had once been hers.

Gran! He and she had always had a love/hate relationship. Once he'd been her biggest fan, in awe of the simplicity, directness and magical plotting of her work. But as he grew older and began writing himself, her stories seemed too simplistic, moralistic and stereotypical – although, as he would be the first to admit, he would still hang on her every word.

"Show rather than tell," he'd once had the audacity to suggest to her, as though he'd been addressing his undergraduates.

"I've never heard of a story *show*-er, Mark, unlike a story*teller*," she'd replied. "And if I might suggest something in return, Mark. Less head, more heart."

The comment had hit home for, amongst his collection of rejection notices, criticisms of his prose for being arid and soulless were not unfamiliar.

All of this was currently of concern to Mark, for he was shortly to catch a plane to New York to meet with a publisher who, following an award Mark had recently received, was interested in putting out a collection of his work. But the boss of Wine Press added that they needed one more original story.

Mark kept quiet about the six years it had taken him to squeeze out the stories they already had. He knew he was a slow writer, and, of course, his academic day job took a lot of his time and energy. This was why he'd been so pleased to have this new piece, even if he was also suspicious about its provenance, arriving with the speed of a pizza delivery.

As his taxi made its way through the busy traffic, Mark decided to give the story a listen, for he found he could hardly remember it in any detail. It was as though he'd been in a trance – not that he held to such superstitious twaddle. It was the sort of thing his students were always after: muses and other inspirational talismans.

Though Mark tried to keep his phone at a low volume, the driver surprised him by shouting back, "Don't keep it to yourself, bud."

Mark was happy to share. It was rare to find his work exciting interest. However, minutes later, he began to regret it. Had his driver just run a red light? Mark also had the feeling that they'd slowed up, as though the man wanted to prolong the journey in order to hear the story's outcome.

The final straw occurred when they almost became a bumper sticker on the car in front. As the car screeched to a halt, Mark snapped off his recorder, despite the driver's protestations. He promised the man he'd send him a copy of the story once it was published.

❦

Things were no different on the plane when Mark again tried to listen to his story. Aside from wanting to hear it right through, other concerns now troubled him. First, it had no title. Unlike Gran, he always liked to have some sort of handle on his stories, highlighting their concerns. She'd maintained that they restricted a story, inhibiting its growth and change. If someone asked her for a title, she'd just say, "Come up with your own."

His other worry was that, currently, his story existed only in oral form. Gran had always carried her tales in her head, but Mark needed something more tangible, fixed in print. Seeing the words also helped with editing, which again was something Gran never bothered with. For her, each performance became a new version. Accordingly, Mark decided that he wouldn't just listen to the story over the two hours he had to kill, he'd transcribe it. And he'd come up with a title.

Although he found it difficult to type with just his left hand, Mark laboriously began tapping the words into his laptop, transcribing it phrase by phrase, repeatedly having to replay sentences. He held the phone in his right hand, close to his ear so as not to disturb fellow passengers.

However, after only a few minutes, the woman next to him politely asked if he'd just play it through. Mark began to explain what he was doing when the man across the aisle joined in. "If you'd let us hear it first, pal? Transcribe it after?"

Mark eventually agreed but laid down one condition. "I'll let you hear it if you come up with a title. How's that?"

They readily agreed, and he turned up the volume. However, only moments later, those in the seats behind requested that it be made even louder. Mark was excited by their interest. He reiterated his condition about coming up with a title, promising an acknowledgement for whoever had the best suggestion.

After restarting the story for the third time, he noticed that the cabin crew had gravitated to his seating area, trying to look busy. Mark could hear call buttons sounding, but the crew seemed unconcerned. He was, of course, flattered at the hypnotic looks on their faces. He felt a power he'd never experienced before.

It was then that he noticed that one of the stewards had his thumb on the intercom button. Did this mean, wondered Mark, that they were listening in the cockpit, too? He was just recalling his eventful taxi ride when the plane juddered and rocked before everyone experienced a stomach-clenching plummet. It might only have been an air pocket, but Mark was not happy. He thought of that phrase people trotted out when reading a good story: "I couldn't put it down." However, if you were piloting a plane at the time, it was less than funny. Mark found himself imagining a headline: Tale spinner ends in tailspin!

Looking around at his fellow passengers, though, what most surprised him was that no one else seemed bothered. They all had that glassy look in their eyes. That did it. Mark hit pause. Within seconds, the protests and groans erupted: "Come on, buddy, put us out of our misery," "Yeah. Don't be a spoilsport," "Press play!" Someone even attempted to grab his phone!

☾✸☽

After his white-knuckle outward journey, he'd thought things were looking up in New York. There'd been a couple of meetings with the Wine Press team before Mr Grossman, the boss, had taken him out to lunch. This, thought Mark, was it, his golden opportunity. When the question of an extra story came up, Mark whipped out his phone and passed it across to Grossman – stressing that the man should keep it close to his ear. He certainly didn't want waiters delivering food into their laps.

Initially, all went well. Mark watched as the story took hold, the next mouthful of Mr Grossman's starter sliding stealthily off his fork. The man sat hypnotised, his mouth agape, his salivary juices no doubt wondering why no more food was forthcoming.

Like a hooked fish, Grossman was reeled in. Mark observed the man's excitement increase, his eyes widen, his limbs start to shake. Unfortunately, what Mark took to be positive signs turned out to be symptoms of an impending stroke. The next thing Mark registered was Grossman going face down into his deep-fried Camembert. Mark quickly extricated his phone from Grossman's hand before someone else spotted it. Waiters soon surrounded their table to conceal this spectacle from other diners.

❧❋❧

Back in his apartment, Mark flopped into his easy chair. He was exhausted. He'd taken the next flight home after his fruitless trip – the book deal having been put on hold.

Half a bottle of whiskey later, he was still in his chair, gazing at himself in the cheval glass. The story, he was convinced, was the jinx. It had already put a number of lives in jeopardy – including his own. That plane flight had been his scariest moment. He kept picturing the plane spiralling down in a fatal tailspin – all thanks to this tale. Could a story cause homicide, he found himself wondering.

Focusing on the mirror, phone in hand, he swung back his arm. However, the pain in his wrist made him swap hands. The resultant, left-handed throw was feeble. The phone missed the mirror entirely, ricocheting off the wall and crashing to the floor.

He might not have broken the mirror, but he'd done a good job with the phone. Its screen was cracked in several places, its innards gaping. Straightening up, he caught sight of his reflection, which had an uncharacteristic twinkle in its eyes.

"And what are you looking at?" he demanded, an insight slowly dawning. Although his busted phone was in his right hand, in his reflection it appeared to be in his left – the hand that he'd used for throwing. And, of course, when he'd first spun his troublesome tale, he'd also used his left hand.

Knowing that another story was on its way, Mark flipped open his laptop and gave his sinister side free rein. But this time, he'd have it in print, starting with the title he'd already decided upon.

The Gibbet Tree

I caught sight of Tom's face, smeared with juice, and burst out laughing. Ostensibly, we were out blackberrying, but we'd also planned to have a look at the fracking site up on Lord Martens' estate. This was one of several sites around the Weald licensed for testing, despite local opposition.

There had already been complaints about earth tremors and loud noises, but Martens had so far managed to ignore the protests. However, there was a meeting scheduled in the village hall in a week or so's time, which he was expected to attend.

Although the location of the site was meant to be hush-hush, all us locals were aware of it and loads of us had gone up to have a look. It was the talk of the school. So, when Gran had promised a blackberry and apple pie if she could find some willing fruit pickers, Tom and I had leapt at the opportunity.

We'd filled our margarine tubs even before we'd got past Farmer Boland's land. It was then we realised what a state we were in, the sweat and juice glistening off us. Aged fourteen, with Tom just turned twelve, we felt rather self-conscious and paused to clean ourselves up before moving on to the summit of Gibbet Woods – as it was known – from where the fracking site was visible.

When we finally reached it, we were amazed. It was as though a giant had snipped a neat rectangle out of the landscape. All the trees and bushes had been removed over an area about the size of two tennis courts, leaving a barren patch of grey soil. A wire fence, topped with barbed wire, enclosed it. There were also floodlights and, inside the enclosure, a Portakabin and some other containers. In the middle stood what looked like an oil derrick.

"Wait till Dad clocks this," I said, taking pictures.

"Should make Martens enough dosh to buy a few more classic motors."

"How many does he need?"

"You're such a spoilsport – just like Dad," said Tom, running back into the woods. I chased him down, playfully thumping him on the back.

As the large trees enveloped us, our cries were muffled, as though we'd entered a church, the green canopy diffusing the light and the spongy earth absorbing every sound. It was like walking on the gym mats in school.

We were approaching the Gibbet Tree itself, an old oak with swollen, arthritic-looking limbs, when the wind blew, and its boughs creaked as though in pain.

Dad had many stories about this tree. In his day, corpses of animals used to dangle from it, hence its name. The victims were meant to send a message to other vermin, warning them not to go near the lord's precious game – his partridge and deer, that is. And, as Dad always said, amongst the "vermin" his lordship included us villagers. There were always skirmishes over rights of way, poaching, foraging and the like. This still goes on, with Martens forever trying to keep us off his land by removing stiles, blocking pathways, letting his animals roam freely and suchlike.

Suddenly, I halted, horrified. "Look!"

"What?"

"There, in the tree," I pointed. "It's a fox, isn't it?"

"Foxes don't climb trees," said Tom.

"No, stupid! Hanging there." I was staring at an orange-red body with a white-tipped tail, swaying in the breeze, its back legs unnaturally twisted.

I thought Tom had also clocked it, but then he shouted, "And there's a crow." The bird in question, just about to settle on the fox's body, flew off at the sound of Tom's voice. "Oh no," he lamented, giving me a hearty shove. "It's alive after all."

"Gerroff," I said, returning his shove with interest. But I was suddenly spooked. "Let's get out of here."

Perhaps my shove was more forceful than I'd realised, for Tom overbalanced and dropped his tub. The lid sprang off and his blackberries trampolined away.

"Idiot!" I said, bending to retrieve the fruit.

But Tom was no longer playful. "Me?" he shouted, leaping to his feet. He was raging, his teeth bared, eyes flaring. "If you hadn't attacked me in the first place."

The next instant, he was on my back, wrestling me to the ground, pushing my face into the soil. Just as suddenly, he released me and ran off. I lay there for several minutes until I heard him return.

"What's got into you?" I began, before realising it wasn't Tom. Involuntarily I shrank from the figure who was scarcely taller than me but looked ancient. His skin was the colour and texture of oak bark. For some reason, I thought of the diddicoy that Dad talked about, who used to live in these woods.

After my alarmed reaction, I tried to be civil. The man had joined me in picking up Tom's berries. "My disgusting little brother's somewhere around," I said, keen that he should know I wasn't alone. I began calling Tom's name as I wandered round the clearing.

I eventually found him, crouched in a little dip. "Sorry, sis," he said. "Don't know what came over me."

"It's this place."

"Yeah," he agreed. "Creepy."

"But I've just met someone really helpful. He's collecting your berries."

Back in the clearing, though, the man was nowhere in sight. All we could see was Tom's margarine tub sitting neatly on the ground. Without another backward glance, we made for home.

When we came to the B312 at the bottom of the hill, Tom ran ahead, having heard the whine of a vehicle approaching at speed. He fancied himself a connoisseur of performance cars.

"Aston Martin DB5 Convertible," he shouted after the car had creamed past. "Top speed 140 mph. James Bond drives one in *Goldfinger*."

"How interesting," I replied. "I presume it was Lord Alfred at the wheel?"

"MARTY 1, yeah," said Tom. "Who else could afford that?"

"Who else would drive like that?" I responded.

Further up the road, the forlorn wing of a long-squished crow waved in the car's slipstream.

❈

At tea, Tom and I were tripping over each other to tell Dad about the fracking site. My photos particularly incensed him and, when Tom decided to stick up for his lordship, Dad became even more exercised.

From the sidelines, I was quite enjoying their head-to-head until I mentioned the Gibbet Tree, at which point I was appalled to hear Tom deny what we'd seen.

"It was just some old kite blowing in the branches," he claimed.

I couldn't believe it. "Why are you being such an a-hole?" I demanded, storming off to my room.

Dad came up later, carrying a slice of Gran's pie as a peace offering. Under Dad's spell, I was soon my old self again. He was in one of his nostalgic moods and began telling stories about village life when he was a boy. I always loved listening to his tales, even if, as Gran was quick to point out, half of them were actually about his *dad's* childhood.

I asked him about the diddicoy. They were brought in, he said, by Alfred's father, Percy, who'd managed to alienate most of the local workforce. The diddicoy were tinkers and travellers who were just passing through, but Lord Percy invited them to stay, offering them the run of his woods "and all the hedgehog pie they could eat" if they'd help with the running of the estate. "He thought he was getting cheap labour – and a private army, no doubt. But the diddicoy weren't as biddable as he'd hoped."

Over time, many drifted away, but a core had remained into the 1960s, when Dad was a boy. Then there had been an accident involving one of the diddicoy lads – a contemporary of Dad's – who was found hanging in the Gibbet Tree.

I knew the story well. It was the source of many a tall tale at school. Of how the lad's ghost haunted the tree. Of how people who went up there at night disappeared, only to be found weeks later, off their heads.

Dad was always dismissive of such urban myths. He wanted people to pay more attention to the facts and injustices of the case, especially, as he once again reiterated, the verdict of the inquest: "death by misadventure."

"Somehow, this boy manages to wind a rope round his neck while swinging through a tree, and hangs himself!" proclaimed Dad for the umpteenth time. "No one thought to question young Lord Alfred, though. Although all his teachers were well aware who the lad's tormentor was."

I found it hard to imagine Dad and Alfred as classmates, but it had once been so, before his future lordship was whisked off to his exclusive preparatory school, "to avoid contamination from us plebs," as Dad liked to put it. Of course, nowadays Alfred didn't acknowledge any of his childhood pals.

Although I'd heard this story many times before, I now felt more invested in it. "Didn't the whole diddicoy clan turn up for the hearing?" I asked.

"They did indeed, Suze. And after the verdict, they upped and left. A long convoy of them there was, many still with horse-drawn wagons. We lined the streets to show our respect. Never seen the like." Dad shook his head at the memory. "Many curses were mouthed that day."

I thought again of the strange figure I'd encountered. I wasn't exactly sure what a diddicoy looked like, but I thought my stranger fitted the bill. I almost told Dad about him but, for some reason, decided against it.

After the day's excitement, I was surprised at how well I slept. Tom, as I learnt at breakfast, was not so fortunate. Not only had he been plagued by nightmares about beasts hanging from trees, but he had the gall to blame *me* for feeding him such scary ideas!

"Sure the beasts weren't just kites?" I asked him, as I left for school.

☾✹☽

A few days later, on my way home, I was convinced that the whole village – not just Tom, as I'd originally thought – had gone mad. Some of my best friends were acting most peculiarly. It was hard to put your finger on it, but everyone was edgy, tetchy. The fracking activity

– the booms and vibrations – seemed to be doing people's heads in.

The tests certainly divided village opinion. A sizeable minority was in favour, hoping to benefit in terms of jobs, but the majority resented the intrusion of outsiders with their destructive machinery, especially knowing that Lord Alfred was behind it all.

Disputes raged in the local press and on social media. At the weekend, Dad witnessed "a pitched battle" outside the Red Lion between pro- and anti-fracking groups. We all hoped that the village meeting might cool heads, although the intended presence of Lord Alfred (no doubt accompanied by his legal team) didn't fill anyone with confidence.

At least, said many locals, Lord Percy had some commitment to the village, "even if he was an aristocratic knobhead" (these were Dad's words). Alfred, by contrast, was "just a waster, an absentee landlord who enjoyed the playboy lifestyle."

He only came back to the village, it was said, to play golf on his exclusive course, which he'd created after having some tied cottages demolished, making homeless a number of local people. The wildlife, which lost much of its habitat, also suffered, as the amount of roadkill on the B312 showed. Alfred had even tried to appropriate some of Gibbet Woods when he'd had his course laid out, to give it a challenging bit of rough. But local opposition had been resolute and his lordship had had to revise his plans.

Many suspected that this fracking venture was his revenge. If so, he might have got more than he bargained for, as news of the row had spread far beyond the village. Aside from the golfing community, national environmental groups and media crews had become involved, sensing a good story.

The atmosphere was febrile, even in our own home. Tom and I were continually at loggerheads and Mum and Dad were little better. Had Tom really not seen that fox in the Gibbet Tree? I wanted to go back and check. And I was also keen to see if that strange man was still up there. Was he really a diddicoy?

Tom, though, wouldn't consider another trip. His nightmares had put him right off. I was set to go on my own, but Dad was also keen to see the fracking site, so we went together, walking along the bridleway that ran parallel to the B312. Along the way, we met up with a couple of Dad's old schoolmates, Jim and Mac, who were also keen to see what was going on. The three of them were soon reminiscing about their schooldays with Alfred. Jim told us about how he'd once been invited to Martens Hall, to celebrate Little Lord Alfred's sixth birthday.

"Quite a do," Jim said. He'd been particularly impressed by the animal remains everywhere. "Mounted heads covering the walls and skins all over the floor – tigerskins, bearskins and that." Jim said Alfred had his own collection of taxidermy in his bedroom, with animals and birds dramatically posed in glass cases and domes. "There were hawks, hedgehogs, weasels, sparrows, rabbits, mice, foxes – anything, in short, they'd killed. Of course, the diddicoy had done the stuffing. Talented lot."

The three old boys had become so absorbed in their reminiscing that they'd bypassed the Gibbet Tree and walked straight to the fracking site. I peeled off, agreeing to meet Dad later.

❦

Even before I reached the tree I encountered the diddicoy again, dressed in the same ragged clothing with his shirt buttoned tight at the neck. I approached him gingerly, for he didn't seem to hear me and I could see he was upset. "You alright?" I touched his shoulder.

He stood up and stretched out a hand, revealing a fluffy ball of feathers. With his other hand, he parted the plumage to indicate an airgun pellet. He spoke with a guttural twang that made him hard to understand, but his gestures more than compensated.

We made our way across to the Gibbet Tree. Even from this distance, I could see that not only was there definitely a fox hanging there, but several other corpses had now joined it. In fact, one of them was the crow I'd seen mangled on the B312, its intact wing a giveaway. Like the other bodies, it had been artfully positioned. While some of these corpses, like the crow, were recognisably roadkill, there were other casualties, such as a shrew still trapped in its drink-bottle coffin.

As we reached the tree, the diddicoy, ancient though he looked, nimbly scaled the trunk. He was soon above my head, spreading the wings of the small bird he'd been clutching, angling its neck upwards and holding it in place with some wire.

I suddenly realised that all these creatures weren't *vermin* at all, but *victims*. The diddicoy was commemorating them. It wasn't a Gibbet Tree but a Commemorative Tree.

Noticing that it was now dusk, I began to look around for Dad. He was nowhere to be seen. I waved goodbye to the diddicoy, still aloft, and started for home. It wasn't long before I saw Dad, heading my way.

"Find anything else in the old tree?" he asked.

"Not really," I said, not sure why I was being so evasive, sounding more like Tom.

"I thought I saw something move up there."

I could discern that faraway look in Dad's eyes.

"You've been tattling too many tales," I replied, borrowing one of his phrases. "Let's hope Gran's saved us some pie."

After that, we talked of nothing but the fracking eyesore.

☾❋☽

I woke the next morning to feel my bed shaking. I suspected Tom of trying to waken me in some unsubtle way, but discovered I was alone. I went down to tell Mum and Dad, but they'd also felt the tremor. There'd been an item on the radio, they said, with callers-in demanding that tests be halted.

At school, there was a continual sense of menace, perhaps brought on by the tremors. In the playground, I watched a gang of boys career round, arms joined, knocking down anyone in their path, yelling, "The frackers'll 'ave ya!"

The day was a nightmare. As soon as the final bell sounded, I escaped and ran for home. Everyone I passed looked either distracted or angry. Car drivers were particularly unpredictable, locking horns as they encountered each other. I was extra careful crossing the roads.

After a hasty evening meal, during which no one spoke much, I made my excuses and went for a walk. Normally I'd ask permission, but not that night. I just needed to escape. The air was heavy and oppressive, as though a storm was on its way. It was only when I approached the spot where the bridleway crossed the B312 that I began to relax. Despite the tug of vehicles on the other side of the trees and bushes, the bridleway remained peaceful.

Ahead, I could see a pheasant about to make his ungainly way across the road. Stupid bird! I knew what was going to happen but could do nothing to prevent it.

I could hear a car looming. Surely the driver must have seen the bird on the verge? Surely the driver would … slow down?

I broke into a run which, I realised in retrospect, might have made things worse. The bird, perhaps spooked by my movement, vainly tried to take off, launching itself straight into the path of a flashy Mercedes.

I recoiled as the pheasant, now a lifeless lump, bounced back onto the verge. The car sped on. No attempt at braking, no attempt to discover what had happened. MARTY 4, proclaimed the numberplate. I might have known!

I ran to the bird and picked up the warm body. There didn't seem to be any blood but it was dead. Although I hadn't intended to go up to the Gibbet Tree that evening, I now felt I had a reason. I was sure the diddicoy would be there.

Sure enough, there he was, standing by the tree, hands raised. The clearing was electric with energy, which he seemed to be conducting. Seeing me, he ran over and gently took charge of the pheasant. I tried to explain its fate.

Reverently, he cradled the bird and, muttering, carried it to the tree. I did a double take. The tree's branches were now festooned with bodies, displayed like strange fruit. Apart from those I'd seen earlier, I could identify weasels, rabbits, hedgehogs, blackbirds, thrushes, sparrows and more. But they no longer appeared dead. Although their eyes must have been pecked out long since, each socket looked alive.

There were also older remains adorning the branches, which the breeze was spookily animating. Skeins of translucent skin rose like miniature kites on frames of bone and sinew. Tatters of feather, tufts of fur and hair fluttered like ragged bunting; and bones clattered and clacked one against another.

Were these remains all returning to life? I wasn't sure, for the clearing was also humming with flies, bloated things that were starting to register my presence. There was a rotting smell, too. A thick, sweet odour that settled in my throat, making me gag.

I watched in fascination as the diddicoy gently pinned the pheasant to a branch, spreading its beautiful brown wings as though the bird were still in flight, as though it had soared clear of the Mercedes' bonnet.

A minute later the diddicoy was back down the tree and, with his knife clutched between his teeth, he approached me. Straight at me he came, and, seizing my wrist, pushed me towards the tree. I was suddenly terrified. Was I the next exhibit?

Before I could protest, I felt a stinging in my palm. Looking down in disbelief, I watched as my lifeline welled. I was as helpless as the pheasant. Tears sprang to my eyes. Perhaps I'd end up alongside it!

But the diddicoy was gentle, his hand a supportive tourniquet about my wrist. In his other hand, he held a bowl into which he was channelling my pulsing blood.

Some sort of voodoo? I thought of home, of poor Tom, of my warm bed. What was I doing here?

Then the air stiffened and the wind rose. The bones weren't simply clacking now. The wind had turned the marrowless tubes into whistles, which squealed and hummed with sound. The ligaments of the older bodies were starting to vibrate, adding a bass thrum. Was the fracking causing this, possibly?

No, I thought, looking at the diddicoy. This was the man in charge. He stood at the base of the tree, armed with a switch of twigs, using them like a brush to flick drops of blood – my blood – over the ragged assembly of creatures.

It was this action that was making their bodies shake and twitch, as though galvanised. The more he bloodied them, the more animated they became. Now they were twisting and gyrating, tugging at their bonds. I looked on, horrified, as the beady eye sockets started glowing inquisitively.

The diddicoy put down his switch and turned to me. I feared the worst, but his movements were reassuring. He took my hand and rubbed some sort of paste into the cut, which immediately staunched the bleeding. He folded my fingers into a fist and bound it with cloth. It throbbed. Did I need stitches? Would I have a scar?

I had little time to consider, for the noise in the clearing was building to a crescendo. I watched the entire assembly of beasts begin to climb into the night air. No matter that some of these creatures – the hedgehog, the weasel or the rabbit – had never flown. They rose regardless, flapping and clattering, whistling and shrieking.

I suddenly recalled that afternoon's English lesson. We'd been studying collective nouns – murmurations, exaltations and the like – and I found myself struggling to think of an appropriate term for this swarm: an orchestration? A reincarnation? Such terms were still churning through my head as, above me, the swirling mass of fur, feather, skin and bone seemed to orient itself and, with a shrieking, clattering sound, disappeared into the night.

As this sound died away, I became aware of other noises rising from the village. The diddicoy gave my injured fist a final squeeze, then gestured for me to leave. I didn't need any encouragement and ran all the way home, albeit with a feeling of exhilaration rather than fear, as though I too had been uplifted by this "reincarnation".

Several times on my journey I had to avoid groups of locals who also seemed infected by the madness of the night. Armed with sticks, knives and bottles, they were roaming the village, not quite sure what to do, but keen to dissipate their pent-up rage.

As soon as I was home, I announced my return and went straight to my room, my head swirling, my palm throbbing.

The cut was only superficial and seemed to be healing almost magically, thanks to the salve the diddicoy had applied. I protected it with a rubber glove and took a shower. I was filthy. Then I popped my head round the lounge door and said good night.

☾✳☾

The following morning, I awoke surprisingly refreshed. The pain in my palm was the only thing untoward, a reminder of the craziness of the previous night. But for this one piece of evidence, it might all have been a dream – or perhaps one of Tom's nightmares.

I could hear a commotion in the kitchen. I dressed and went to join the family. The local radio was on, as usual, with everyone glued to it.

"Some lads attacked the fracking site last night," said Dad. "Vandalised it." He sounded quite proud of them.

"What have you done to your hand, Suzie?" asked Mum.

☾✳☾

At school, many were boasting of big brothers and sisters who'd supposedly been involved in trashing the site. But such talk was soon overshadowed by more serious news, that of the death of Lord Alfred Martens. The head, looking suitably downcast, came to each class to announce that "Our illustrious benefactor has met with a fatal accident."

Only later did more information emerge and, even then, many suspected that much of the story was still being suppressed. Officially, his lordship was said to have suffocated, though it was admitted that there was also extensive laceration to his body, mainly from broken glass – glass that had come from the splintered cases containing his lordship's extensive collection of stuffed fauna and flora.

The police initially suspected that those responsible for vandalising the fracking site had paid his lordship a visit, but there was no evidence to support this. It was hard, though, to discern what had really happened, for the village was incandescent with rumour.

Staff working at the hall had reputedly found stuffed beasts from the cases splattered all over Lord Martens' bedroom. Some of the birds' beaks were said to have been embedded in the walls, other creatures blocked the chimney and some, it was claimed, had even been found in his lordship's bed. As for Alfred himself, his oesophagus was said to be choked with feathers – causing his suffocation – while his skin had been flayed with claw and bite marks.

The way the glass cases and domes had been broken, claimed Dad (information he gleaned from some of his mates), it looked as though the stuffed beasts had burst *out* of their containers – which, as Dad added, was quite impossible.

"A reincarnation," I said to him.

A few days later, I went back up to the wood with Tom. We were now talking again – as was everyone else. The whole village seemed more at peace with itself, as though a storm had cleared the air. Even the Gibbet Tree looked healthier, with new shoots sprouting. As for the fracking site, it had been mothballed. With Lord Alfred gone, no one knew its future.

🌙

Pending a post-mortem, his lordship's funeral was delayed by several weeks. The service and interment were then held at the local church, where the family had its tomb. It was well attended, but few amongst the mourners appeared to be well-wishers. To everyone's surprise, some travellers also put in an appearance, though they kept in the background.

I kept a lookout for my mysterious friend. I wanted Dad to meet him. I'd almost given up when, at the end, as people were departing, I saw the man's diminutive figure. He was dressed in his regular garb, except for a bright neckerchief that he now wore around his neck.

He proffered his hand. After my ordeal at the Gibbet Tree, I was nervous of responding. But all he did was turn my palm up and run his finger along my scar, now barely distinguishable from my lifeline. If anything, the line itself looked more robust.

"Nais tuke," the man said, a smile lighting up his face and then, more haltingly, he said, "Thank you." Then he walked off.

As he retreated, Dad turned to me. "You'll never guess who he reminded me of."

But I already had: "A reincarnation."

Milton Keynes UK
Ingram Content Group UK Ltd.
UKHW040817141124
451205UK00001B/20

9 781738 442225